"**H**OLD REAL STE loose. The gun w shot."

She nodded, redistribi and tensed up.

"Relax."

"I am relaxed."

No, she was strung tighter than a bed rope, but he knew better than to say so.

"Close one eye." Even looking straight ahead as he was, he could see the cute way her eye squinted shut, her mouth puckered in concentration. Almost like a kiss.

She fired. The rifle stock struck her shoulder, knocked her backward and into him. The cut length of tree trunk spun as it fell. His arms came about Millie's middle like he'd done so a hundred times, the most natural thing in the world.

He tried to keep his eyes on the log to judge her shot, but found the woman snuggled against him far too distracting.

"I hit it! Did you see that?" She spun in his arms, her face turned upward to his. Satisfaction glittered in eyes an impossible blue. "I *hit* it!"

"Yes, ma'am. That you did." He found himself smiling in response to her delight. Early morning sunlight illuminated her youthful skin, so pale compared to his own, so enticingly feminine. He needed to trail a fingertip along her jaw, if only to assess its softness, so he clenched his fingers in the worn calico of her dress to keep from touching her skin.

Her mouth drew his attention as plump lips parted. It would be so easy to lower his head and steal a kiss. Interest, something a whole lot like desire, flickered in her eyes and he simply *knew* she'd had the same thought. His gaze slid lower, returning to lips he ached to taste.

Why did it feel so good to hold her? He didn't want to like it, didn't want to feel this pull toward a woman who wasn't Abigail. Sure as sunrise, attraction for his secondhand bride was *not* part of the plan, ran counter to their agreement, and definitely not a good idea.

Nothing had changed. He *still* didn't want a wife—just a help meet. Given her abusive son-of-a-bitch husband still lived, John couldn't be more than a stand-in husband and he'd do well to remember that.

Published by Kristin Holt
Copyright © 2014 Kristin Holt, LC
www.KristinHolt.com
ISBN-13: 978-1499370614
ISBN-10: 149937061X

Book design by Kristin Holt: www.KristinHolt.com
Cover Design by Elaina Lee, www.ForTheMuseDesign.com

This book is a work of fiction. Names, characters, places, and incidents are products of the writer's imagination or have been used fictitiously and are not to be construed as real. Any resemblance to persons, living or dead, actual events, locales or organizations is entirely coincidental.

All rights reserved. No part of this book may be reproduced, scanned, or distributed in any manner whatsoever without written permission from the author except in the case of brief quotation embodied in critical articles and reviews.

Dedication

For Diane Darcy. You are an outstanding mentor. Thank you.

GIDEON'S Secondhand BRIDE

A Sweet Historical Mail Order Bride Romance Novella
(Rated PG)

by
KRISTIN HOLT

GIDEON'S *Secondhand* BRIDE

A Sweet Historical Mail Order Bride Romance Novella
(Rated PG)

The last thing John Gideon wants is another wife.

Mere weeks have passed since John buried his wife, but he must trudge forward. For the sake of his three little ones, he has no choice but to remarry. His mail order bride must agree—this marriage will be strictly business.

Permilia is desperate to flee the bonds of marriage...

The War Between The States cost Millie her kind, gentle husband. He came back in body, but his soul was ravaged by war. To save herself and the life of their toddler son, she leaves her abusive husband though she has nowhere to go, no money, no family. A single option surfaces—a farmer has sent for a mail order mother, housekeeper, and helpmeet. It's a marriage in name only, so she justifies disappearing into the west and keeping her secrets.

...a marriage her husband vowed she'll never escape.

Oliver Owens warned Permilia the only way she'd leave him would be through the undertaker. It's only a matter of time before he catches his runaway wife.

He doesn't want a wife.
She doesn't want a husband.
Marriage of convenience?
Perfect.

Chapter One

Harrisburg, Pennsylvania
October, 1870

MILLIE'S HUSBAND HAD NOT DIED in the War Between the States.

But oh, how she wished he had.

Moonlight trickled through the only window, casting a long shadow over Oliver Owens's prone body—diminished, weak, and emaciated from a steady diet of liquor. His rage had finally run its course, leaving him unconscious.

Unfortunately, still breathing.

Millie shivered in the cold. Pain seared through her ribs and she held her breath, both arms tucked tightly to her battered body. With no fuel to burn, their rented room had grown frigid after sunset.

The tenement's paper-thin walls provided little privacy; she heard someone's baby cry, footfalls on the floor above, her empty stomach rolled at the odor of cooked cabbage and onion. How many neighbors must have heard Oliver's rage, the beating, her cries, and chosen to do nothing?

Each breath blazed like fire within her damaged ribs. Her right eye had swollen nearly shut. The pain was intense enough to block the ever-present hunger pangs. An empty old orchard bottle weighed heavily in her numb grasp, solid as any club.

Think you'll leave me, woman? The undertaker will carry you out.

If Oliver lived, he'd make good on his threats. She clutched the glass bottle, helpless rage building within her. The tides had turned—now *he* was the defenseless one. Fury shook its way free of her soul, lending her strength she didn't have, power to bludgeon—

Glancing toward the baby's pallet, she saw young Oliver had awakened. He silently watched her every movement with wide eyes. Two years old and already so learned.

Her precious son deserved a chance to live without constant fear. But did that desperate hope justify *murder?*

Her heart tripped in its rhythm even as her posture sagged. She couldn't do it, couldn't kill the man she'd once loved, simply didn't have it in her to fight brutality with violence.

The bottle slipped from her fingers and thumped against bare floor boards. The thud mingled with the din of dozens of families in this miserable tenement. She swayed on her feet, dizzy with pain and hunger.

Oliver slept on.

She could see the inevitability now, the long road stretched behind with every choice that had brought her—brought *them*—to this point where she had the strength to leave him. Not sure where she'd go, having nowhere to turn, penniless and defenseless, she gathered her son and meager possessions.

She would leave, permanently, for any fate would be preferable to the hell of living Oliver Owens. He would *never* strike her again.

AT BEST, MILLIE HAD A TWELVE HOUR head start. Oliver *would* come after her, and he'd start with Clara Walker—the closest thing Millie had to family, her best friend, her only refuge—a woman whose husband fought alongside Oliver in the Infantry, wore widow's black, and mourned. Clara deserved to be forewarned.

Gentle rain fell from a leaden sky, soaking her through

in the short distance to Clara Walker's home. Crisp night air cut through Millie's wet clothing and chilled her to the marrow.

She snuggled young Oliver closer, his tattered quilt bundled tightly about him. He sniffled and tucked his wet cheek against her neck. She kissed his brow and murmured words of encouragement intended more for herself than him.

Desperate to get out of the weather, for even a few minutes, Millie slipped down the shadowed alley to Clara's kitchen door. The house was dark, yet three quick raps brought Clara to light a candle and lift a corner of the curtain.

Clara opened the door quickly, pulling Millie and son inside. The kitchen smelled of fresh bread and simmered beef causing Millie's stomach, so long empty, to cramp with hunger.

Instant concern registered in Clara's brown eyes. Her warm fingertips touched the swelling flesh at Millie's cheek. The cold night had a numbing effect but Millie couldn't help but flinch. Her son snuggled closer, his little arms locked about her neck.

"Oliver struck you." Clara's lips compressed in a tight line of disapproval.

What must her friend think of her, that she evoked such anger in her husband? That their marriage had crumbled, despite her efforts? Millie nodded as tears filled her eyes.

Clara urged Millie to sit, quick to notice the wince she tried to hide.

She couldn't meet her friend's gaze, so she dropped her tattered sack of sparse possessions to the floor beside her chair. "I've left him." A sob broke. "I'm here to warn you. He'll come here first, searching for me when he wakes."

Clara pressed a cool, wet cloth to Millie's abused face. Her long dark braid fell forward over her shoulder. "I'll be ready." Her tone softened. "I'm not sorry you came to me."

She locked the door, took a pistol off the shelf and set it within reach. "And I'm not sorry you left him. I may be too bold to say so, but you should have left him long ago."

Clara stoked the banked fire in the cook stove and put a

kettle on to boil. She set an abundance of food on the table before Millie. Bread. Cold beef. Cheese. Milk. Apple slices.

More food than Millie had seen in weeks.

How often had she sat at this table, especially in the early days after Oliver's return, sharing tea and a meal while he worked? Of late, he'd not allowed her to go out.

Millie ate. It was easier than looking her friend in the eye. She offered young Oliver a piece of cheese. "Eat," she urged. He shook his head and clung more tightly.

Clara bustled about, toweling Millie's hair, wrapping a dry blanket around her and young Oliver, hanging the little boy's quilt over a chair to dry by the heat of the stove.

Millie unbuttoned and offered her son her breast, grateful yet again that her milk hadn't failed. The babe's survival had too often depended upon her nourishing him.

Her stomach complained after consuming only a small portion of the offerings. How long since her last substantial meal? A week?

Clara poured heated water into a bowl and sponged Millie's abrasions with a clean cloth. The ministrations felt so good, the kindness a sharp contrast with all she'd endured. Tears stung her eyes and she blinked them back.

As their tea steeped, Clara finally spoke. "You cannot stay in Harrisburg. If you're within reach, he'll come for you."

"I know."

"Where will you go?"

She couldn't quite meet Clara's gaze. "My mother's cousin, in Vermont." A distant relation Millie had never met, who may or may not still live, a woman whose connection to Millie was tenuous at best.

"Oliver knows of this cousin?"

"No." Millie slowly shook her head. "I can't recall mentioning her."

Clara's hand settled over Millie's. "How will you get the two of you all the way to Vermont?" No censure in the question, just concern and practicality. In Clara's gaze, Millie could see she considered the dangers of a woman traveling alone with a toddler, the great distance from Pennsylvania to Vermont, and Millie's obvious lack of money.

Millie shrugged one shoulder, bracing her battered ribs. Without money, she had no choice but to rely on the compassion of strangers, to beg a ride as far as someone might be going. She knew Clara's savings to be meager. Even if her friend offered, Millie couldn't take her funds.

Clara's brows drew together. "I know just the thing." She knotted the sash of her wrapper as she hurried to the parlor, returning with a folded paper. "This is perfect. You will disappear to the Kansas frontier, evade Oliver forever. No one else knows about this man as his request just arrived today. It's not yet recorded."

Oh, no. She knew exactly what Clara proposed, and Millie couldn't do it. Clara supported herself working for Mr. Trudeau's Mail Order Matches, an agency that connected brides—often war widows or orphans—with lonely men in the territories. Business thrived; the west had a significant dearth of women and war-ravaged States too many.

Clara must've seen the immediate rejection on Millie's face because she pressed onward. "Listen to me, Permilia Owens." The slender, petite woman she'd trusted and loved like a sister had a presence much larger than her person. "This is the *only* way. Do you want to die? Do you want your son to die? You cannot return to Oliver, you cannot stay near Harrisburg or he will find you, you haven't the means to travel the distance to a cousin who may or may not take you in, and this is the *only* way."

Sadly, Millie knew that was true. Her tears increased. She hated those tears—such a sign of weakness. "I cannot present myself as a mail order bride."

"You can. You're an orphan. You have no family, nowhere else to go."

"I can't—I'm married." Not a happy state. She rued the day she'd wed Oliver Owens. "How could I lie?"

"You can't get a divorce—it's too hard to come by, the process arduous. You'd have to stay here, indefinitely, and there's no guarantee your suit wouldn't be laughed out of court."

Clara spoke the truth. Millie had no hope of legally dissolving her marriage—no money, no connections, and the physical abuse wouldn't be enough to earn a judge's good favor—everyone knew that. How many times had she alternately wished Oliver dead or daydreamed the possibility of divorce?

Millie wilted in the hard kitchen chair. The law might force her to remain married to Oliver Owens, but could not make her stay with him. She *would* leave. Just as soon as she'd rested and eaten. She'd walk as far as possible, beg a ride from passing travelers, perhaps ride in the back of a merchant's wagon as far as allowable. If she couldn't reach Vermont and her only relative, perhaps she could find somewhere else to hide from Oliver.

"I hear divorces are easier to come by in the western territories." Clara placed a gentle hand on Millie's shoulder. "More than not, I suspect, people just start fresh."

"I *can't*."

Clara's expression softened as she took a seat beside Millie at the kitchen table. Her soft grasp on Millie's hand felt soothing, companionable, more kindness and affection than Oliver had shown her in ages. "It happens all the time. Men and women alike. They leave their life in the States behind and simply disappear into the territories or California or Mexico and don't look back. Take up new names, new histories, present themselves as someone else. Who's to say different?"

Clara sighed, held Millie's gaze for a long moment. "Not everyone who takes a new name is running from the law. Some, like you, simply *must*. Self preservation."

"I can't marry again. It's not legal, not moral. Most of all, I don't *want* a husband—not Oliver and not anyone else. I want to be free."

Marriage had imprisoned her, worn her threadbare, broken her soul.

She held young Oliver close, his little heart beating beneath her hand. He'd finished nursing. Her damaged ribs screamed as he pushed away. This precious babe had been the only good thing to come from her ill-fated marriage.

Millie buttoned up. No, she definitely did not want a husband nor marriage. Marriage did not mean protection, safety, and needs met—marriage equaled incarceration.

"I've read his letter, Millie. John Gideon is not looking for a wife, not really. Just a companion to care for the children. Most specific in his requirements, actually, he requires his bride to be a mother already."

Clara pressed the letter into Millie's hand. "He sounds like a kind man. I think this fellow is worth taking a chance on. He's more worried about his kids, willing to take on a stranger to care for his little ones, when most men would've farmed out the children to other families so he could grieve in peace and quiet or return to work unhindered."

Clara sighed. "You may remember that's what Dr. Elliott did, and he could have afforded, easily, to hire *two* nannies to live in and care for his twins. I don't know if he'll ever call those children home."

Millie opened the letter, curiosity about this man taking root.

"He offers marriage, protection, his name." Clara drew a deep breath and met Millie's gaze. "And train tickets west."

Chapter Two

Dickinson County, Kansas

"MUCH OBLIGED, MR. FARNHAM." Millie accepted his offered help to step down from the buckboard. Her cracked ribs screamed in protest but she refused to allow her new neighbor to see her flinch. Young Oliver's little body seemed both heavy in her trembling arms and painfully light.

Her knees nearly buckled as her feet touched down. Had she ever been so weak? She'd not eaten in two days, and her son, since yesterday. He was too little to go without. She'd sold her wedding ring back in Greensboro for pathetically little, and the proceeds had fed them for a few days.

Her milk, which has been all that had seen young Oliver through the hungriest of times, had failed her during the journey. He may be old enough to wean, but the inability to nourish her hungry baby broke her heart.

When she'd inquired in Abilene as to where John Gideon lived, she'd been lucky to meet David Farnham. A friend of Mr. Gideon's, whose spread was roughly two miles further out. He'd offered the ride she desperately needed. She'd not had the strength to walk the remaining six miles.

David Farnham had chattered as the wagon rattled along, filling her in on all the news he'd picked up in Abilene. She'd learned John's three young ones were cared for in town until his mail order bride could arrive—and how no one expected the agency to get a bride out west so quick.

Farnham glanced up at the log house he'd identified as John Gideon's as it had come into view. The land stretched, flat as could be, for miles in every direction. So few trees, compared to home. Incessant wind kept the worst of the afternoon heat at bay, tugging on her skirts and drying the perspiration on her back.

The simple structure seemed solidly built, a good four or five times larger than the rented room she'd shared with Oliver. Glass windowpanes looked dusty and the porch needed a good sweeping. A chicken coop, small barn, and a covered well surrounded the house. Not far away, two trees flanked the necessary.

Home. This welcoming place, this security, would be her home. Relief swept through her, followed close behind by gratitude.

"He's in the field," Farnham said. "Likely won't be in until dark."

"I figured so." It was better this way. She'd been hungry for so long her thoughts weren't sticking together. She needed food and to wash up after the journey, to make herself and young Oliver as presentable as possible.

She had no trouble making herself at home in John Gideon's cabin.

After all, his letter had laid it all out. She'd read and reread his neat penmanship, explaining the business arrangement he required. Propriety demanded marriage, but it was a business deal, plain and simple. And for her part in raising and educating his children she and her child would receive safety, a home, support.

Young Oliver needed that support *now*. Frankly, so did she.

Mr. Farnham shuffled the reins. His gaze lingered on her face, on the bruises that must still show. "John Gideon's a good man, gentle and kind. He'll be good to you and your young'un." He shifted on the seat, his gaze now hesitant to remain on her face as he broached the subject he'd ignored during the long ride out of Abilene. "You look like you need a bit of kindness."

Millie's cheeks flushed hot with embarrassment she couldn't suppress. Memories of Oliver were so very close to the surface. Guilt flooded her, washing its stain from crown to toe. She hadn't come to terms with the decision to consign her old life to the past and forge a future for herself and young Oliver, lies and all, as John Gideon's bride. In that moment, she doubted she ever would.

This was wrong—she presented herself as something she was not, taking advantage of Mr. Gideon's train tickets and good faith, his support and kindness. She would eat his food, sleep under his roof, care for his children, illegally wed him—and keep her secrets.

Shame made her feel dirty, past her battered and grimy exterior, all the way to her soul.

Mr. Farnham watched her a little too closely. "You all right here by yourself?"

Millie swallowed her self-contempt. "Yes, Mr. Farnham. Thank you for your help."

He watched her closely for another long moment, and she couldn't meet his gaze.

"Ma'am." He tipped his hat and flicked the reins.

As the wagon rolled out of the yard, Oliver fussed in her arms. His grubby clothing smelled sour, his little face streaked with dirt where tears had dried. Blond hair matted lifelessly to his scalp and his feet needed a good washing. She must appear just as disheveled, probably worse, because of the bruises.

Inside, the cabin was cool and dim, tidy and comfortable with well-crafted table and chairs in the kitchen area and a rocking chair and stool near the hearth.

A single bedroom had been added on, extending the cabin to nearly twice its original size. The bed was unmade and rumpled clothing lay in a heap in the corner. Most importantly, the shelves near the cook-stove were generously stocked with foodstuffs. Fresh milk waited in a covered pail on the kitchen table.

She'd made it as far as sitting down with young Oliver to a simple meal of milk-toast when she heard boots on the porch. Her heart lodged in her throat and she pushed to her feet. Her cracked ribs screeched in protest at the sudden movement. Old panic left over from Oliver—who was now so blessedly far away—surfaced.

Oliver flashed to anger so easily and been impossible to please. He'd grown more violent in the past year. If Oliver found her where she'd not been invited, eating what was not hers, he'd vent his fury without hesitation.

What would Mr. Gideon do?

The door opened and there he stood in a shaft of bright afternoon light streaming in the portal. John Gideon, just as he'd described himself. Over six feet tall, lean of build, light brown hair and eyes a few shades darker.

She noted more, which he hadn't disclosed. That lustrous hair hung in waves well below his lantern-square jaw. Rolled up shirt sleeves revealed forearms muscled from labor and browned from years working in the sun. Suspenders rested on broad, strong shoulders. Perspiration darkened his homespun shirt at the throat and beneath his arms. The very picture of good health.

His eyes were clear, his gaze steady. Despite the recent tragedy of losing his wife in child-bed, he hadn't taken to the bottle. Millie knew, far too intimately, the look of a man who imbibed and John Gideon apparently did not.

Welcome relief relaxed her weary shoulders.

Despite finding an unknown woman and child in his home, eating from his stores, he didn't seem the slightest bit angry. Something like compassion softened the set of his jaw.

He took in the plain brown calico dress in desperate need of laundering, a weary body in want of a bath. The swelling had receded, but the bruises Oliver had left on her face were no doubt still visible.

In that awful moment, she saw herself through his eyes. A dirty, starving woman, battered and discarded. Unwanted. Worthless.

She felt so very small, guilt over her deception warring with humiliation. She doubted her sunburn would mask the heat rising in her cheeks.

She couldn't meet his gaze.

The moment had dragged on, and still he remained

silent. Why wouldn't he speak?

Would he send her away? Where would she go?

She swallowed the dry lump in her throat.

Would he demand answers about the bruises?

Suddenly it seemed even more wrong to pass herself off as a widow. She couldn't lie to him. Coming here had been a wretched mistake.

Gideon's attention had turned to young Oliver. The lad had buried his face in her skirt and refused to cry, even in his fright. She stroked his dirty hair to soothe him.

Millie smoothed over the baby's wet cheek. He'd eaten less than half of the small portion of milk-toast she'd set before him. His spoon remained clutched in his little fist.

She saw the decision settle on John Gideon's expression, but didn't know what it meant.

"David Farnham found me just now. Says you're my mail order bride." Mr. Gideon's voice resonated deep and rough, but not unkind.

Her heart rolled over. He hadn't refused her. Not yet.

"Yes." She bobbed a curtsy, more habit than intentional. "Mrs. Permilia Owens." Her conscience pricked, though she'd intentionally given him her true name. "Millie, if you please," her words came out barely more than a whisper. "My son, Oliver."

She wouldn't think about it; the decision had been made. *I'm free, I'm allowed to start fresh.* After all, Oliver had broken every marriage vow and she'd left him far behind. This would work because Mr. Gideon wanted a marriage in name only. It might be illegal to wed again while her husband still lived, but as Clara had said, Millie wasn't the first to start anew in the west, and she wouldn't be the last.

It had to be done.

She stood a little taller, forced herself to look him in the eye. If he'd accept her, she'd do her part, meet his expectations in a help meet, make sure he didn't regret keeping her. She would bury her guilt deep and never allow it to surface.

Mr. Gideon shut the door, diminishing the light in the kitchen. "You got here right quick. I didn't expect a response for awhile yet, and certainly not a woman before a letter."

Millie pulled out the letter of introduction Clara Walker had hastily written before her departure. "From Mail Order Matches."

He took it and stepped into the stream of sunlight through the dusty window panes. Motes danced in the shaft of light. Seconds passed as Gideon easily read the letter of introduction. Millie had read the letter and knew it contained a list of reasons why Mrs. Permilia Owens was a good match and why Mail Order Matches had selected her as Mr. Gideon's bride.

He nodded. "You read my letter?"

"Yes, sir." He seemed to be asking *if* she could read.

"You understand my expectations?"

He didn't sound hostile, just wary. She could understand that. He'd made himself clear; this would be a business arrangement—the major reason she'd accepted his offer and come west.

"A marriage in name, only," she said. "I'm to care for your three children."

He watched her smooth Oliver's baby-fine blond hair, the wariness giving way to something softer, more like compassion. She guessed his children took priority over the rest of her responsibilities, but she listed them anyway. "Keep house. Cook. Launder. Mend and sew. Tend the garden. Milk the cow on evenings you're late in the fields. Put up stores against winter."

His searching gaze seemed to really take her in, as if he could see through her dusty and weary exterior. A moment passed where she suspected he could through to her perfidy.

Her heart pounded. *Tell him,* her conscience demanded. *Confess the truth.*

Why? So he'd put her out in this rough country, with worse prospects than before? The hunger she'd suffered the last few days urged her to bite her tongue.

With a simple gesture, he encompassed his home, the farm. Almost in apology, as if he knew this snugly built frontier cabin did not compare to fine homes in the East. "Will you commit to stay?"

"Yes." She had no desire to return to Oliver, nor face

trying to protect and feed her son alone. "I will. I do." Already, she could see John was the far better man.

"I won't love you." His statement repeated what he'd written. His request for a mail order bride had not been for a young woman with dreams of romance, plans for love and happiness and the bearing of children.

No. John Gideon had made it clear there would be no real marriage. No love, only a cooperative business relationship. He'd do his part and she'd do hers.

For her, love hadn't worked out well at all. The distant memory of Oliver, before the war, crowded her thoughts. *"I'll love you forever, Mills."*

Forever, it seemed, was woefully brief.

She shook off the unwanted memory and met John Gideon's gaze. "Good. That's exactly what I'm counting on. I won't love you, either."

This arrangement was more than acceptable to Millie—it was perfect. She didn't want a real husband any more than he wanted a wife. This marriage of convenience served her needs as much as his.

John nodded in acceptance.

A genuine smile blossomed, stretching the healed split on her lower lip. She couldn't suppress the hope rising within her.

Ever so slowly, he returned her smile. The lopsided grin tugged at his mouth, making his solid good looks suddenly far more handsome.

They stood there for a long moment, measuring one another. Millie stroked her fingers through her son's hair, relieved he'd begun eating again. With chubby toddler's fingers, he tucked milk-soaked bread into his mouth.

"Eat," he said, then cleared his throat. "Wash up, if you'd like. I'll ride for the pastor and collect my children. I'll be back in two hours."

JOHN STOOD UP WITH MRS. PERMILIA OWENS—Millie—and tried to banish memories of another wedding. Not so long ago he'd wed Abigail with so much love in his heart, such blissful anticipation of their lives together.

He never thought to marry again.

Late afternoon sunlight streamed through the west-facing window and cast long shadows.

"Take your bride by the right hand," Charles Reddick said as opened his bible.

Her hand was so different from Abigail's, with shorter fingers, overall a little smaller. Warmer than he remembered Abby's to be.

Though this marriage was a business arrangement, plain and simple, Preacher Reddick used the same words. The same vows. Same scripture. But everything was so very different. His heart wasn't involved, and never would be.

Behind them, Mrs. Reddick and their son, Frank, served as witnesses. As far as the Reddick family was concerned, this was a happy occasion. A nice, normal wedding. Their daughter Laura, almost a woman herself, rocked the two youngest children while his oldest, Benjamin, played quietly at her feet.

He'd noticed Millie's son Oliver, clean from a thorough washing, sat apart from the others and watched everything. The boy seemed more than shy. Almost as if the kid was scared of the unfamiliar surroundings and people he didn't know.

He glanced at Millie, finding her blue-eyed gaze dropping from the minister's face to his vest, then flitted over the minister's shoulder to the view beyond the windowpanes. Nervousness had her shifting from foot to foot.

He'd been concerned, too, when he'd returned home with his children and he'd taken careful note of her reactions. What mattered was her ability to love and mother his little ones.

She'd taken baby Sarah into her arms as if it were the most natural thing in the world.

She'd do.

He'd liked how she'd sat on her heels to greet Benjamin and Margaret with tender smiles and touches to their brows. She'd tried to hide the obvious physical pain crouching down like that caused her, betraying injuries hidden beneath her clothing.

He'd wanted to know what had happened to her, the words poised on his tongue, but realized the question wasn't one he wanted an answer to, not in front of the Reddicks. Mrs. Owens deserved her privacy. Maybe he'd ask—later—and maybe he wouldn't.

They were turning a new page, both of them, starting a new chapter in their lives. From here on out, he'd take responsibility to protect her. That didn't necessarily mean he had the right to ask intrusive questions about her past. It wouldn't be that kind of marriage. Some things were simply too private for him to discuss with this new wife, and he would extend her the same courtesy.

Obviously, she'd washed up while he'd been gone. Her head of honey-blond hair was still damp, but braided a little and twisted into a tidy bun at the nape of her neck. She wore a long sleeved simple cotton work dress that had seen a lot of wear. The calico had long since faded to a dull, nondescript gray. It must be the best thing she'd brought with her.

She looked so young.

Even younger than she had at his kitchen table when he'd first seen her. And more weary, if that were possible. He wondered, again, how recently she'd lost her husband.

What had happened that she'd accepted his offer?

Desperation. Anxiety. Doubt. He'd seen that much in her gaze before she'd managed to hide it.

Why would she choose a loveless marriage of convenience? He'd think a young, lovely thing like her would want to marry for love.

She'd met his gaze for just a moment, her hollowed cheeks and sunburned skin telling him almost as much as the fading bruise on her cheekbone. Had a ruffian knocked her about, stolen her funds? Women traveling alone were often at the mercy of the unsavory types, especially this far west.

But those bruises weren't new. Looked 'bout a week old.

And hunger wasn't new to her, either. This woman had been poorly fed for a very long while. Bones stuck out prominently on her face, her wrists. She looked like a stiff wind would knock her off her feet. An itty-bitty thing, she barely reached his shoulder, and couldn't weigh more than a hundred pounds.

Guilt nudged him. He should have thought to send traveling expenses along with the train tickets. Not that he had that much cash money to spare. But he should have thought of it.

He'd only been thinking of himself, of what he needed out of this arrangement. A caretaker for his three young children, still babies. He needed someone to cook and clean and mend and launder their clothes...he needed a housekeeper. But a man can't live with his housekeeper, even out here. So a decent offer of marriage had been on the table.

What did Millie need out of this arrangement?

Support, obviously. Plenty to eat. Someone to help raise her son. A father for her child.

The preacher must've asked Millie for her vow, because she murmured, "I do," with a shaky, thready voice.

From the corner of his eye, John saw her swallow, hard. Her jaw clenched tight, and her eyes squeezed shut, just for a moment, but long enough to betray her discomfort and her refusal to look the preacher in the eye.

With a smile and nod, Preacher Reddick addressed John with phrases he'd heard before. Words he tried not to take to heart this time.

He knew a moment's shame at his disappointment that Millie's son hadn't been older, old enough to work the farm with him. In his mind's eye, he'd pictured a widow arriving with three strapping adolescent boys to share his burden.

"Do you take this woman unto you to be your wife?" Reddick asked, not yet expecting an answer. "To protect and care for her, as you would yourself?"

Again, John had been focused on what was in it for him.

He'd allowed it, because it was so much more comfortable than focusing on everything that had gone wrong in his marriage to Abigail. Sweet, soft-spoken Abigail.

Guilt surged, suffocated, hot and as fresh as it had been the day he'd buried his beloved bride.

Charles Reddick cleared his throat. "Will you shelter her, love and honor her, all the days of your life?"

He'd made these selfsame vows to his precious Abigail.

And ended up killing her, vows or no vows.

Not intentionally. But dead was dead.

Guilt threatened to consume him. He swallowed down the knot lodged in his throat.

The preacher wanted an answer.

Millie turned toward him with uncertainty. She blinked, her lashes resting on sunburned cheeks for a moment too long.

Looked like she doubted him, too.

But this time, *this time*, he *would* honor the vow to protect. He forced certainty into his voice. "I do."

He'd warned the preacher they would not exchange rings nor kiss.

John looked into eyes as blue as the sky and shook Millie's hand to seal their agreement.

Chapter Three

ON THE MORNING AFTER the wedding, John arose early to be in the fields by sunrise. He returned from the barn carrying the morning's milk in a tin pail. He inhaled the aroma of eggs and potatoes fried in butter.

His new wife was awake. Up and already working.

So far, so good.

Though he'd come up with the obvious answers, the questions he'd battled with since the ceremony still nagged. What did Millie need from their agreement, and why the bruising?

Near the hearth, Millie cuddled baby Sarah in the rocking chair, wrapped up against the morning chill. Her gaze skittered away from him, back to the baby, where her fingertips caressed his daughter's downy head.

The wash of golden firelight bronzed the pale flesh of her throat, the jut of collarbone, a small swell of breast. His new wife needed to gain some weight.

Millie wore a long white nightgown, her bare toes peeking from beneath the stained hem. One long braid hung over her shoulder, the rope thick and surprisingly smooth. She swept a tender fingertip over Sarah's brow and cheek, an image of maternal devotion that tugged at his heart.

Affection—a warmth he couldn't mistake as anything

else—began in the vicinity of his heart and spread outward.

Abby had rocked their babies in that chair...all of them, except young Sarah. And now Millie sat there, filling Abigail's vacancy, cradling his baby to her breast. Sarah nursed greedily. He'd heard those suckling noises before, plenty of times.

Millie glanced up then, catching him staring. She eased the blanket over baby Sarah to better cover herself from his view.

She might feel a twinge of embarrassment, but he didn't. Nursing a babe was the most natural, most beautiful thing he'd witnessed, and would forever bring Abigail to mind.

Grief kicked hard and fast, stealing his wind and lodging a fist-sized lump in his throat. He missed his beloved wife with a desperation that seemed it would never leave him.

He couldn't look at Millie any longer, so he pulled the towel off his breakfast plate and picked up his fork. Despite the grief that tore at him, the food smelled appealing and his mouth watered.

He forced himself to take a deep breath, then two. He'd be all right. Things were looking up. He'd been surprised—and grateful—last night when he'd overheard Millie talking with the preacher's wife about leaving his infant daughter here with them. Asking for a bride who was both a mother *and* had not yet weaned her own babe hadn't even crossed his mind when writing to the agency.

Because of Millie, his baby girl had spent her first night under his roof. All three babes at home, a gift—his family, as whole as it would ever be.

He forked a first bite of egg and potato. He chewed, forced it down past the dissolving lump in his throat even as he realized his breakfast tasted good.

"You need to know my milk was failing when I arrived here." The chair he'd built for Abby rocked back and forth, back and forth. "I'm hopeful my milk will return and be good for her, but if it doesn't, and soon, we'll have to take Sarah back to town."

He met her gaze, concern banishing the remnants of grief. "How long 'til you know?"

"No later than tomorrow. But I'm hopeful...now that I'm well-fed." Gratitude and humility colored her words. "Thank you."

He nodded. It seemed mighty odd she'd thank him for basic support as such was every wife's due. Again, he wondered how long she'd been fending for herself, how long she'd been alone.

He finished his meal, set his plate and fork in the dishpan. He brought a chair from the table to sit opposite Millie.

She looked up from Sarah's face, met his gaze. For just a moment, she seemed worried. Almost frightened. But the expression passed quickly.

"It seems to me," he began, "I'm getting everything out of this arrangement I needed. I realized I don't know what *you* need from our agreement. So I'm asking."

A moment passed, the chair rocking gently, the wooden runners creaking. Sarah sighed and must have released the breast, for Millie closed her nightgown modestly. The baby stretched her little limbs in the safety of Millie's arms.

Millie, this new wife he knew so very little about, put his daughter to her shoulder and patted her little back.

"I need only what you offer." She still wouldn't meet his gaze. "You've given me your name. You've taken me in and given my son a place. That's all I need."

He'd thought of all that, yesterday. But now, seeing Millie this skittish, there had to be more. He'd get to that part, later, when Millie was ready, but first, he had an apology to make.

He leaned forward on the hard chair, braced his elbows on his knees. Linked his fingers together loosely. She pushed against the floor, rocked forward, pushed again.

"I apologize for not sending money for your journey." Two or three full meals later, the guilt wouldn't subside. He'd done wrong by her, and still, she worked diligently to fill his daughter's belly.

"Mr. Gideon..."

He looked up then. Offered a half smile. "John." Asking her to call him by name was not a breach of their agreement. They needed to be comfortable with each other. God willing, they'd be living side by side for a good long while. "Call me John."

Surprised to find her looking directly at him, he held her gaze for a moment. A gentle smile caught her lips and awareness tingled within him. This world-worn woman was lovely. Nothing like Abby's golden beauty, but pleasant just the same.

"John," she murmured, at last looking away. At the baby, at the fire in the hearth, anywhere but at him. "No apology necessary. Your train tickets made it possible for us to travel. Without that support, I couldn't have come."

He nodded. Her answer was enough for now. But why had she wanted to come west? When had her husband died? Who had mistreated her? The bruises stood out in harsh relief in the golden wash of firelight.

"I see you need clothing. Oliver will need shoes before winter." He'd seen the child's bare feet. Her dresses were threadbare and too insubstantial for the cold months ahead.

He'd seen the meager bundle of belongings she'd brought with her. She would need new shoes to replace the heavily worn pair she owned.

She didn't answer, so he pressed forward. "It's been a few years since my wife, ah...since Abigail sewed much." Why was it so hard to talk about Abigail, whom he had loved—whom he *did* love—with the woman who'd come here *because* of Abby's death?

The rocking chair stilled. Sarah's breaths slowed in sleep. Millie still didn't answer.

He glanced up, finding her studying his face. He clenched his interwoven fingers more tightly, aware he danced around the issue, and didn't like himself for it. Some things simply had to be said.

"A lot didn't get done around here in Abigail's last years." As her illness progressed, she'd lost more and more strength. "She was weak of constitution, felt poorly, since our first babe was born silent."

"I'm sorry."

The compassion in her voice registered in her eyes. She *did* understand. She'd lost her husband, hadn't she? Surely she comprehended the gaping void left by Abigail's death, by the lost promise of that first son whose life ended before it had begun.

"I'll buy the cloth we need. You'll sew for yourself and Oliver, too."

She nodded, eased the baby from her shoulder and proceeded to rub her back and pat her face, apparently trying to wake the babe. Didn't she want Sarah to sleep a few more hours?

His surprise must've shown because she said, "My milk was almost dried up. I believe it can be restored with frequent demand." Her gaze lowered again. "I *will* feed your baby."

He tried not to watch while she got Sarah to take the other breast, kept the little one awake by rubbing her feet while she suckled. He found he trusted her, this woman he barely knew, to nurture and protect his infant daughter. All his children.

Gratitude mingled with respect.

It would be a great deal easier to work the fields, knowing Millie had things well in hand at home. He'd worried something awful over Abby, who'd often been too weak to get out of bed, much less care for the children.

"Thank you," Millie said softly, "for the cloth. I'd be happy to see you and the children outfitted for winter."

"And you," he reminded. It was easier to talk about clothing than about his past with Abigail.

"Yes." Her smile caught him off guard, a beautiful smile that showed even, white teeth that overlapped just a little in front. "And me."

He felt like a foolish young pup, grinning back at her. Without love, couldn't he foster companionship?

"If Mrs. Gideon wasn't able to get much sewing done," the replacement Mrs. Gideon asked, "how did you get by?" She gestured toward his clothing, a finely made shirt and brown vest he'd bought in town.

"I paid a tailor in Abilene. It'll be nice to avoid the hassle of going all the way to town to place an order, carry the kids in for measurements, pick it all up." He meant to express his thanks for the work she'd agreed to do, for saving him the cash required to pay for the work to be done elsewhere, but wasn't saying it right. He settled with, "Thank you—I'm grateful you sew."

Her expression betrayed her disbelief. "Every woman sews. It's a key homemaking skill."

"Maybe." He didn't need to sully Abby's memory by divulging that sewing—something she could have done even after she'd been mostly confined to bed—hadn't been her strong suit.

So he changed the subject. "You need to eat. As much as your body will take until you regain your weight." He'd seen how her two dresses hung loose on her frame. "I won't have it otherwise."

She nodded, lowering her gaze in apparent embarrassment.

"I *need* you to recover your health." His voice snagged on that last word. He felt an urgency to explain that Abigail's health had failed, as Millie deserved to know, but now wasn't the time. Emotion ran too high, too thick. He couldn't find the words.

While he worked to tamp down the tide of emotion, Millie looked up. He held her gaze for a long moment, one that stretched time to an unnatural crawl. In her beautiful eyes, he could see she comprehended his sorrow, the pain of loss and the awful truth.

Some things were better left in the past.

MILLIE FOUND SETTLING INTO LIFE as Mrs. John Gideon brought a contentment she'd never known in all her days as Mrs. Oliver Owens.

John spent every moment of daylight working the fields, planting winter wheat. He was home only long enough to eat his supper, wash up, and fall onto the pallet he slept on in the main room. He would rise long before daybreak, eat the hot breakfast she'd prepared while he did chores in the barn, and be on his way.

They hardly spoke, except about the children and the most superficial of subjects. Just as his letter to Mail Order Matches had stated, the single bedroom was hers to share with the children. Millie found that was just fine with her.

Because he was comfortable. Yes, still a stranger, but a stranger who'd shown her nothing but kindness and decency. A stranger who'd given her a fresh start, provided food and shelter and safety for herself and her son. He'd easily earned her trust. It was all far more than she could've said for Oliver.

Every time thoughts of her former life surfaced, she buried them deep, urging them to fade right along with her bruises and healing ribs. She couldn't think of Oliver—that life was her past, dark memories she wouldn't allow to overtake her here. So she focused on caring for John Gideon's children and home; a fair trade for all he gave her in return.

On the afternoon of her fifth day as Mrs. Gideon, the little ones napped in the bedroom. It had taken her this long, but the house was scrubbed top to bottom, bringing a rewarding sense of satisfaction in a job well done.

Fresh bread cooled on the table and a stew she'd prepared for supper simmered on the stove. The mingling aromas contributed to her sense of wellbeing.

Enough food, for the first time in years. A husband who treated her with courtesy. A safe place for her son to grow up. Young Oliver had started smiling and he played with the eldest of Mr. Gideon's children, Benjamin, who was only a few months older. Seeing the boys play without concern or fear brought a sense of peace that filled her heart to overflowing with gratitude.

John's middle child, Margaret, a year and a half old, had taken to Millie readily. The little girl was happy, good-natured, and cooperative. Her curly blond hair formed a halo around her cherubic face, a lovely contrast to brown eyes, so much like her father's. She would be a beauty.

Millie wondered if she resembled her late mother.

If so, no wonder John had fallen in love with Abigail.

Millie had no delusions—she knew herself to be plain. Her own mother may have thought her an attractive youth, and before the war, Oliver had thought her lovely.

But the war had changed her. She wasn't pretty, not anymore.

Rain fell from an overcast sky. Just a drizzle, bringing with it a welcome coolness. The wind had settled down, so while the four children napped, Millie set to churning butter from cream gathered from the last four days' milking.

The repetitive motion of churning felt good. *She* felt good. Relaxed. Content. A light breeze gusted past the house and ruffled the few standing trees. Raindrops tapped a patter on the roof and pocked the puddles forming in the dooryard. Such a soothing sound. Hens clucked in the dooryard where they pecked for insects.

Everything was so quiet here, so serene. No constant barrage of voices, clatter of wagon wheels, passing carriages in the street. No ring of hammer against anvil. No neighbors to be heard through paper-thin walls in a dwelling housing fifty families. And no screaming husband wielding fists to teach her a lesson.

She couldn't recall a time when she'd felt this much serenity.

"Hello, the house!" A familiar man's voice caught her attention as a wagon came into view around the bend in the road. She quickly recognized their nearest neighbor, David Farnham, who'd given her a ride from Abilene the day her train arrived.

He waved in greeting and she found her smile quick and easy.

She left her churn and stood at the edge of the porch, out of the rain. "Hello, neighbor."

"Settling in?" he asked, his expression kind. Rain water sluiced off the brow of his hat. In this gray weather, his dark brown hair seemed nearly black. His beard had been trimmed since the day he'd delivered her to John Gideon.

"Yes. Thank you."

He tied the reins around the brake, jumped from the wagon, and approached. He pulled a letter from his shirt, folded about with familiar pale rose stationery and sealed with red wax. Millie recognized it instantly as Clara's. What a joyous surprise!

"I was in town to the blacksmith's and stopped by the mercantile." He passed over the letter. "John's had me collecting his mail for him, and he for me, whenever we get in there."

Clara's flowing script addressed the letter was addressed to Mrs. John Gideon.

"Things good here with your family?" Caring neighbors

checked on each other. Had to, with so few people spread so far and wide.

"We're well. You?" She fingered the letter she hadn't thought to receive. It seemed so like Clara to follow up, to check on her friend. But so soon? This must've been mailed mere days after Millie left Harrisburg.

"Can't complain. My wife says we ought to have you and yours over for Sunday dinner. If not this week, then next."

Lightning forked in the distance to the east, followed by a low rumble of thunder. She thought of John. Where had he said he'd be working this morning?

The storm had caught Farnham's attention, too. He scanned the horizon, the sky, but his stance remained relaxed, his hands splayed on hips. He didn't seem too worried, so Millie pushed the concern away.

What had he asked? Yes, about Sunday dinner.

"I'd like that." But her thoughts were still on Clara—who'd sworn she wouldn't confess to Oliver that Millie had even been there that fateful night. Clara, who'd written so very soon after Millie's secretive departure.

Was something wrong?

Dread seeped in. Slow and chill at first, but rapidly making her shiver. The breeze carried falling raindrops to dampen her dress and press the cold deep.

She'd imagined Oliver showing up at Clara's home or at the Agency demanding his wife and son. Clara had convinced Millie she could effectively lie and would never disclose the truth.

Clara had promised she'd keep herself safe.

But Clara had never known Oliver's particular brand of persuasion.

Millie fingered the letter, anxious to tear it open, to read, to assure herself Clara was all right and her secret remained safe. Her heartbeat thudded loudly in her ears making it harder to concentrate on Mr. Farnham's conversation.

"How 'bout this Sunday, then? Get the chores done, and head on over to our place, plan to stay the day. Grace and the kids are anxious to meet you."

"I look forward to meeting them. I'll pass along your invitation to Mr. Gideon," she assured him, gesturing over her shoulder. "Thank you for delivering this letter. I'll get back to my churning."

"Nearly forgot." Farnham hurried back to his wagon, bringing out several paper-wrapped bundles. Sodden with rainwater, the paper had darkened and tore under his grip. "These are for you. You'll want to hang them up to dry, right quick."

She took the bundles, immediately registering their contents.

"Cloth," Farnham confirmed. "John had me pick it up. Said you had some outfitting to do for the family."

"Thank you, Mr. Farnham, for the delivery and the invitation."

"You're welcome, Mrs. Gideon. I'll be on my way." He climbed onto the wagon seat. "Goodbye, now."

It was all Millie could do to make it inside and drop the sodden packages on the table before breaking the seal on Clara's letter. She opened it with trembling fingers, immediately recognizing her worst fears.

He knows, Clara wrote in imperfect, rushed handwriting, scrawled onto the paper as if she'd been in desperate haste to make the post. *I swear I didn't want to tell him. He came to my home—I refused to answer the door.*

Millie dropped onto a chair. Nausea churned in her gut. Another lighting strike brightened the eastern sky and a rumble of thunder answered.

The scene played out in her mind's eye: Oliver's drunken demands, his fist pounding on Clara's kitchen door.

He came to the Agency. Spoke to Mr. Trudeau, who knows nothing. Intentionally, no record of the transaction. I thought we were in the clear. I'm so sorry, Millie. Please forgive me.

Her handwriting became even more uneven, more frantic.

He can be most persuasive.

Oh, dear God. What had Oliver done to Clara?

Fear spiked, her pulse climbed, and her body flushed hot and cold all at once. She scanned the rest of the letter. She simply had to know the worst of it.

Millie, he knows precisely where you are. He knows you're with John Gideon. You must prepare for the worst.

Chapter Four

MILLIE PACED PAST THE KITCHEN WINDOW for what seemed the hundredth time. The sun's rays slanted at a sharp angle as night approached. The rain had tapered off hours ago, leaving the vegetation glistening and the air heavy with humidity.

She'd barred both front and back doors, kept constant vigilance from each window, and strained to hear sounds of an approaching rider. There was still no sign of trouble, but Millie's racing heart didn't seem to understand that.

She'd been sick twice since obtaining the brief letter, reading far more into the missive than Clara had actually penned. In Millie's mind, Clara had broken bones, teeth knocked out, blackened eyes. Guilt fairly consumed her.

Worse, Millie had put John Gideon and his babies in very real danger.

Oliver would be furious. Enraged. Vengeful.

John had no idea the severe trouble headed this way.

She'd fed the little ones, but hadn't been able to choke down even a bite to eat herself. Her stomach roiled with fear.

To think she'd actually felt safe here. Out in the open where she thought she was hidden, so far away from her husband and his temper. She'd slept soundly, certain Oliver would never find her.

Why had she thought she could escape him?

He'd warned her the only way out would be through death; why hadn't she accepted that as truth?

But she knew why—young Oliver. Their little boy deserved so much more from a father. She'd left Oliver for their son's sake, a decision she wouldn't reverse. It had been the right choice.

Now he knew *precisely* where they'd hidden.

She simply must tell her new husband the truth. All of it. She no longer had the choice to deceive him. Not when he and his precious babies were in danger.

With one more glance out the window and seeing no sign of anyone approaching, Millie dropped to the floor where the children played with their toys. She hugged the three oldest tightly, kissing their little heads indiscriminately. She'd been charged with protecting them, with mothering them. And she'd brought this threat to their very door.

"Mama," Benjamin called, dropping his blocks and pushing to his feet. "I thirsty."

Millie poured an inch of cool well water into Benjamin's cup and gave it to him.

"Me, too." Young Oliver tipped his cup to drink.

Miss Margaret needed more help, her gulps loud. She plunked the cup down on the table. "Up." She raised two little arms toward Millie.

All it had taken was for young Oliver to call her Mama and the others had followed right along. John had even referred to her as Mama when speaking to his children briefly—and Millie found she relished the endearment.

Holding Margaret close, she looked out the windows again. Panic agitated her such that she couldn't sit still.

Not for the first time, the urgency to flee, as she'd done on that fateful night, came over her. Desperation to put distance between Oliver's wrath and herself, to take their son somewhere he could never find them, swept over her. This time she'd tell no one where she'd gone. He would not be able to follow.

But she couldn't. Any woman with a conscience would not leave these helpless babies without protection while their father worked in the field. Nor could she take them with her—they weren't hers, whether they called her Mama or not.

There would be no escaping it. Even if she had the means, she couldn't leave John to face this coming evil without warning.

She simply had to confess everything, though she had no idea how he would respond. Their conversations had been so few, simple, superficial. Would he be angry? Would he rail and yell, berate her for bringing this disaster upon his family?

With anxiety this severe, she couldn't bear to wait the hours until he would return, but she could not go to him, either. Not with four little ones and no way to carry them so far.

She had no choice but to wait for John's return, when she could confess everything. Until then, she had to find a weapon to defend herself and the children, and pray the *good papa* would get there first.

JOHN TRUDGED THE LAST FEW STEPS from the barn to the darkened house. Exhaustion had nearly overcome him, and he'd considered sleeping under the Cottonwood at the edge of the northwest field. But temperatures were dropping, the sun-drenched heat of the afternoon long forgotten, and more rain threatened.

His greatest reason, he grudgingly admitted to himself, was the fact he hadn't wanted to worry Millie. He'd prefer not to think of her in the same way he'd thought of Abigail, as a concerned wife at home, but there it was anyhow.

His muscles complained, but he knew the satisfaction of a completed day's work. Finally, that northwest field drilled in winter wheat, and none too early. Today's mild rains were an omen that fair weather wouldn't last much longer. He could not risk losing the seed to a downpour.

A great yawn overtook him as he pulled off his dirt-caked boots and left them on the porch. He tried not to make any noise coming into the house as he didn't want to wake the children—or Millie. She'd looked so tired when he'd left that morning.

Caring for four babies under age three couldn't be easy on a woman, especially one as underfed as Millie. He'd been glad to see her cheeks looking a mite bit less hollow already.

He reached for the latch, intending to let himself in, silent as could be, but Millie opened the door for him. Either he wasn't as quiet as he'd thought or she'd been watching for him.

"You're still awake," he mumbled, even as a big yawn stretched his jaw until it popped. He scrubbed a palm over his burning eyes and turned to set his lunch pail on the table, but she took it from his fingers.

A low fire of coals warmed the room, but didn't cast off much light. She'd unrolled his pallet in the corner, ready for him to drop onto. He noticed she hadn't drawn the curtains over the windows like she typically did, but was too weary to think it through. Besides, she'd said something and his sleep-muddled brain had missed it.

"Pardon me?"

"I've been waiting for you," she said, steering him to a chair at the table. "We need to talk."

His eyes watered. He rubbed them to clear his blurring vision.

"Sit," she urged. "And eat while I tell you what happened today."

He simply wanted to drop into bed, too far gone to eat. But hunger gnawed at his belly so he uncovered his plate and sat down, started shoveling food without tasting it. He found himself propping his head on one fist, just to hold it up.

Millie took the chair next to his. "I have news."

He nodded, but kept his gaze on his meal, intent on tucking the rest of it away so he could collapse into bed. Already his mind focused on the morrow and the long hours he'd have to put in to get the northern acreage drilled.

Another yawn, this one longer and impossible to halt. He rubbed his eyes with his palms, fighting to stay awake. He forced himself to focus, to pay attention. He couldn't have her thinking he didn't care about this news, whatever it was. "News?"

Millie shifted on the bench, her skirts brushing his trousers, dirty from the field. It seemed odd she was still dressed. Most nights she was in her nightgown before this hour.

She spoke, but her words barely registered. He nodded, just in time to catch his lolling head before it hit the table and prop it back on his fist.

She'd said something about a letter David had dropped by. "Hmm?" It was all he could manage. He pillowed his head upon his arm. Stretched over the table. Just for a few minutes while he listened to her story.

"...letter from my friend Clara..."

She was worried about something. The letter. That's right.

But then the letter was caught on the wind and tugged out of her grasp. She chased after it, but never could catch it. He watched her, frolicking in a green meadow, with wind-tossed grasses to her knees. Her long, golden-brown hair hung down her back, smooth as silk. She turned back, smiled at him in a way that tugged at his heart.

Even though he didn't want to, he liked her smile.

"Go to bed," he heard her urge, tugging him toward bed.

He'd lost this battle, his body too exhausted to stay awake for a few minutes, to listen to whatever it was Millie had to say. He'd make this up to her, tomorrow.

"Into bed with you." Millie's voice.

No. Not the bed he shared with Abigail. The pallet. On the floor in this room.

Abigail was dead. Lost.

He'd never share that bed with Millie.

He dropped to the bedding, rolled to his side for comfort. She settled the blanket over his shoulders just as sleep dragged him under.

SIX SOLID HOURS OF SLEEP did little to alleviate John's weariness.

Morning came far too early. As the family still slept, he ate a couple slices of yesterday's bread and a thick wedge of cheese, hurriedly packed his lunch pail, and slipped out the back door. No sense waking her. Given how late she stayed up last night, she'd be as tired as he.

His vow to make it up to her, to listen to her story about a letter from home, resurfaced. He'd fallen asleep last night—when she'd wanted companionship. Tonight, he'd see to it he arrived home earlier and spent time with her before bed.

He sat on the front porch to pull on his dirty boots. The sky was still dark, only a faint hint of morning's first blush on the eastern horizon. Yesterday's rain left the world smelling fresh and new.

Despite bone-deep exhaustion, he felt such peace in moments like this. The beauty of unspoiled land, the satisfaction of working his own bit of earth and providing for his family.

Such times he felt Abigail's loss most acutely. They'd planned this dream together, the homestead and farming, raising their family under the wide-open prairie skies. How he'd loved her, and still did. He looked to the east of the house, where a marker he'd carved stood on her plot, a mere two hundred paces from the door.

He'd not visited her grave since marrying Permilia Owens.

An emptiness yawned within him. He'd go this morning. He'd sit quietly near all that was left of Abby and remember.

All that remained were memories. And three beautiful children who had their mother's pale hair and brown eyes.

And that thought brought a deluge of guilt raining upon him. The emotion weighed so heavily, tears burned. Sweet beautiful Abigail, whose life ended too soon, whose joy in the birth of each new addition to their family had been so short-lived. Given the opportunity, he'd wish them childless, because that meant she'd probably be with him still.

The door opened behind him just as he stood. He didn't turn. Even in the dark, he sensed Millie behind him, knew she'd approached on silent feet.

"I'm relieved you're still here." Her words rushed out in a torrent. "I was so afraid you'd already gone."

He didn't like the anxiety in her voice. He turned, pangs

of loneliness for Abby shelved for the moment. "What is it? The children?"

"No." She took one step closer. Her pale nightgown reflected a hint of sunrise, sharp contrast to the darkness around her. A long braid lay over one shoulder. She looked so young and fragile.

A long moment passed, as if she struggled to find words. She reached a hand to touch him, seemed to think better of it and folded her arms together. He thought he saw her shiver in the cool morning air and noted her toes were bare on the boards beneath her feet.

Finally, she broke her silence. "I tried to talk to you last night, but you fell asleep the moment you sat."

He waited, foregoing the apology that quickly formed on his tongue—she had more to say.

"A letter came. From my friend Clara, at Mail Order Matches. The one who gave me your letter, introduced us." Her voice trembled. Her words were rushed, anxious.

Something was quite wrong. This wasn't the calm, confident, and reserved woman he'd come to know over the past days.

He couldn't stand there watching her struggle any longer. He'd move them back inside, but feared their voices would wake the babies. He settled for the next best thing. He pulled off his coat and put it around Millie's shoulders, buttoning the top to keep it closed. She murmured her thanks and snuggled deeper into its warmth.

Chilled air sapped his body heat, but nothing turned him as cold as Millie's reticence to speak her mind. This wasn't like her. Suddenly, he couldn't exercise patience a moment longer. Was she having second thoughts? Did Millie intend to leave him, return east? She couldn't—she'd made vows. His children needed her. *He* needed her.

"Letter?" he urged.

She shook herself, pulling out of some deep thought. "Yes...I don't know how to confess this." Tears choked her voice. Her distress tugged his heartstrings.

"Just tell me. Spit it out. I can't help if I don't know what's wrong."

"My first husband," she began, her voice constricted

and oddly high, as if tears were painfully close, "came home from the war—changed, broken in spirit and mind, no longer the man I married."

War had a way of doing that to the best of men. John knew that.

The sky lightened a few degrees, illuminating tears in Millie's eyes. "He'd lost his humanity, I think." She drew a constricted breath that caught on a sob. "He turned mean, vindictive, drank more and more. He beat me."

John's jaw tightened and his fists clenched. How could any man strike a woman? Especially a woman he'd taken to wife, vowed to protect and cherish?

She looked away as if ashamed. "I had to protect our son."

Before John thought it through, he reached for Millie and then she was in his arms. She fit herself to him, her hands tucked up beneath her chin as she snuggled against his chest.

It felt awkward to put his hands on her back, but he did. So very different from Abigail—smaller, shorter, but somehow more solid, even in her malnourished state. It felt so wrong to hold this other woman.

And yet it felt so good. She filled the emptiness gaping within him, banished the lingering loneliness.

"He threatened to kill me. And young Oliver—I *knew* he'd do it. I left him that night. I *left* him."

The bruises. It made sense, now, why she'd come to him with fading bruises and half starved, frightened and desperate. Reality slugged him, hard, a kick to the teeth. "He's still alive?"

She made a strangled mewling sound as she fought to hold in her anguish, panic, and heart-wrenching agony. Twice she tried to speak, finally merely nodded against his chest.

John's pulse thundered, trying to soak in this unwelcome revelation. His wife, his Millie, still legally married to someone else. A brute, who'd caused her unspeakable pain. He remembered how carefully she'd moved those first few days, how she'd favored her ribs. *Damn* him!

Protectiveness flared and he found his arms tightening

about Millie. If that sorry excuse for a man were here, John would show him what pain fists could inflict.

It took a strong woman to protect herself and her son by walking out, taking her chances on her own. His esteem for Millie rose a notch.

"He knows I'm here, John. He knows *exactly* where I am. He knows your name."

That scrap of news struck John, a second hard-hitting kick. "What?" He put Millie away from him, her shoulders in his hands. He searched her face. The barest trace of bruising still shadowed her eye and jaw. Stunned, whether by news she'd come to him not widowed, as he'd assumed, or from the realization that an angry, unstable man may well threaten his family, he didn't know.

How could he possibly protect four small children and this fragile woman from such a threat?

A long moment passed. Millie apparently couldn't bear the silence. "I'm sorry, John. *So* sorry."

His mind raced and fear congealed in his stomach. They were exposed here on the porch where anyone lying in wait could see them. It wouldn't take much to hit the target of her pale nightgown as the sky lightened. He scanned their surroundings, searching for anything out of place.

"I'm sorry I deceived you." Her words distorted with anguish. "I rationalized my lie, knowing our arrangement was only business. It might not be legal to marry again without divorce or death freeing me from the likes of Oliver Owens, but I didn't know what else to do. I had no money, only one distant family member to turn to—*if* she'd have us—more than four hundred miles from Harrisburg. Other than that great aunt, I had *nowhere* to go, no way to feed myself and young Oliver." She cried openly now, her remorse brutally honest.

"I justified the deception because you didn't want me as a *wife,* just a housekeeper and caregiver for the children. I told myself I was only doing what I had to do. To save myself and my boy. I'm sorry I lied to you—you deserved better."

John swallowed hard. Protectiveness rose within him, to defend and shelter. Even with the truth on the table, Millie, his not-legally-wed-wife still relied on him for protection, for safety. The truth couldn't change that. He didn't *want* to change that.

A knot of apprehension churned in his gut. He searched the hulking outline of the barn, black against the slowly lightening sky, for any signs of movement. His gaze darted to the corral, then the trees swaying in the breeze on either side of the necessary.

No sign of unwanted company. At least not yet.

"Please," she begged so low he could barely hear her. "Say something."

She searched his face with such intent, he couldn't bear it. So he pulled her to him once more to hide the indecision that certainly registered in his expression. He understood her motives, and now her reasons for accepting his business proposal of marriage made a great deal of sense. *This* was what she needed out of marriage to him—a place to hide from her abusive husband.

Compassion wrestled with much weaker sense of betrayal, the battle proving short-lived. Compassion won. "He forfeited his right to you, the moment he struck you, and when he failed to provide for your most basic needs."

She stood so stiffly in his embrace, her anguish unmistakable. He had to reassure her, even if he couldn't make it all right, couldn't fix it. He would not put her aside just because her first marriage hadn't legally ended—they both had their reasons for agreeing to this marriage of convenience. "We won't speak of it again. He doesn't affect our agreement. I won't drag your good name through the mud just to get a circuit judge to sign off on a divorce."

In his arms, Millie stilled, seemed to freeze solid. He expected her to draw a breath, but she remained immobile. "Millie? Do you understand me?" He splayed a hand over her back, his bulky coat insulating the contact.

She nodded, the barest of movements.

He needed her to understand. "Nothing has changed between you and me. As far as everyone in Abilene and the surrounding county is concerned, we're married all official-like and no one knows any different. We signed that marriage license, the ceremony was properly officiated and recorded."

She must've heard him this time, because she slowly

relaxed in his arms.

"As far as I'm concerned," he said, "God sees us as married, and that's good enough for me."

"You sure?" she asked, muffled against his shirtfront.

She seemed to expect the worst—anger, accusations, threats, and that chased away any lingering hint of betrayal. Of course she expected the worst—after marriage to Oliver Owens, how could she anticipate anything else? But John thought that by now she'd know him better than that.

"I'm sure," he vowed. "We won't speak of it again. It doesn't matter."

Now that was settled, they had bigger problems to contend with. Oliver Owens, damaged by war, knew where his wife and son had gone. And that wife apparently feared he would follow.

If she suspected he would follow, bent on vengeance, John had to believe the other man would come.

Here, to where he'd sheltered her.

To his home.

Where his children, mere babies, lived.

That was the crux of it.

In that moment, all John's priorities shifted significantly. The planting could wait. No way could he leave her now, unprotected and alone with four little ones. "Go inside. Get dressed," he urged her, squeezing her tightly for just a moment, "We have preparations to make."

Her breath caught on a hiccup as he released her. She nodded, gratitude and relief in her expression as she went inside.

He *would* see to his family's safety, starting with ensuring Millie's ability to handle a rifle.

Chapter Five

"CAN YOU SHOOT?" John didn't like the idea of his woman unable to handle a rifle.

Millie looked up from baby Sarah, nursing at her breast. Her milk had come back, and his baby swallowed greedily, almost purring as she gulped. "Yes."

She didn't sound as confident as he needed her to be.

After they finished feeding the children breakfast, John said, "Come with me."

Outside, he scouted their surroundings for any hint of trouble while she spread out a quilt and set the warmly dressed little ones to playing in the sunshine behind them. Millie wore Abigail's shawl that had been stored in the trunk at the foot of their bed. He'd told her to make use of anything she found there.

He walked her through the basics of handling his rifle, aiming, firing.

He'd noticed her trembling since she'd confided the danger his family was in, the truth of her past. She'd been hesitant to meet his eye. But her shoulders were square and her chin high. The woman had courage, he'd give her that.

She held the rifle, unsteadily, but aimed just like he'd shown her, sighting down the barrel at a log he'd stood on its end, fifteen paces away. Evidently, her experience was inadequate. He could fix that.

"Squeeze the trigger," he urged.

She squealed at the report. And missed the mark by a good ten feet.

The noise and her exclamation made the two youngest bawl. Oliver toddled over, wrapped his arms about his mother's knees and hid his face in her skirts. John noted the tenderness in which she touched her son's head, how easily she offered solace.

Already, she'd been good for his children. As he'd actually been present for breakfast with his offspring, he'd noticed how comfortable she seemed with them, how well they responded to her. As if they'd always been hers. A woman who nurtured like that shouldn't have to defend herself with a gun.

He hoped it wouldn't come to that.

Just the same, he'd see to it she had the ability and skill.

"Like this," he suggested, taking the rifle from her to demonstrate. "Elbow up. Close one eye and look right down the barrel." He'd been shooting so long, it all seemed second nature.

She watched his stance closely. "I see."

"Try again." He handed over the Enfield. "Show me you remember how to reload."

Her hands shook as she took a paper cartridge from the pouch he'd hung over a fence post. She took the weapon from him, set the butt on the earth at her feet, tore off the paper top and poured black powder into the barrel.

She glanced up, evidently seeking approval.

He nodded. "You've got it. What's next?"

She seated the unused end of the paper cartridge into the barrel, uncertain how far to push it in but seemed to gather her bearings. She tore off the paper cylinder, apparently relieved the bullet rested where it should be.

It took long moments to disengage the ramrod. With several taps, she rammed the bullet home. He judged it to be fully seated against the powder. She slipped the ramrod back into its holder and raised the musket to peer down the barrel.

He fished a cap out of his pocket. Held it out to her.

"I forgot." Her shoulders slumped.

Seemed his wife had some serious self-doubt. He could fix that, too. "You're doing fine. You'll get this." He waited, palm open.

Slender fingers pulled back the hammer, removed the spent cap. Her fingertips brushed his palm as she claimed the cap, leaving the spent one behind. She seated it on the nipple with more care than strictly necessary.

"Take aim."

Nodding, she gripped the rifle. Concentrated a little too hard on how to hold the piece. Took a far mite too long sighting down the barrel. The tension in her posture would throw the shot.

He palmed both of her shoulders. "Loosen up." He jostled her a little, feeling her slight frame ease just a bit. Standing behind her, he extended one arm, pointing down the length of the barrel at the log midst prairie grasses. "Got it in your sight?"

"I think so."

She smelled good. Like sun-dried cotton and freshly-washed hair. He hadn't realized how near he stood until her skirts brushed his trousers. It seemed too intimate to be this near. As with their embraces that morning, it seemed they'd crossed a line. From two people with a bargain to something more.

He felt the familiar strains of guilt building to a crescendo. He didn't want to enjoy touching Millie, didn't want to forget their agreement, certainly didn't want to forget Abigail. Sweet Abby, who still held his heart. Abby, whose shell lay buried a hundred paces away.

He ignored the sensation of this little woman tucked up against his chest, focusing on the task at hand. They had work to do.

"Hold real steady," he spoke at her ear. "Stay loose. The gun will buck, but fighting it throws the shot."

She nodded, redistributed her weight from foot to foot, and tensed up.

"Relax."

"I am relaxed."

No, she was strung tighter than a bed rope, but he knew better than to say so.

"Close one eye." Even looking straight ahead as he was,

he could see the cute way her eye squinted shut, her mouth puckered in concentration. Almost like a kiss.

She fired. The rifle stock struck her shoulder, knocked her backward and into him. The cut length of tree trunk spun as it fell. His arms came about Millie's middle like he'd done so a hundred times, the most natural thing in the world.

He tried to keep his eyes on the log to judge her shot, but found the woman snuggled against him far too distracting.

"I hit it! Did you see that?" She spun in his arms, her face turned upward to his. Satisfaction glittered in eyes an impossible blue. "I *hit* it!"

"Yes, ma'am. That you did." He found himself smiling in response to her delight. Early morning sunlight illuminated her youthful skin, so pale compared to his own, so enticingly feminine. He needed to trail a fingertip along her jaw, if only to assess its softness, so he clenched his fingers in the worn calico of her dress to keep from touching her skin.

Her mouth drew his attention as plump lips parted. It would be so easy to lower his head and steal a kiss. Interest, something a whole lot like desire, flickered in her eyes and he simply *knew* she'd had the same thought. His gaze slid lower, returning to lips he ached to taste.

Why did it feel so good to hold her? He didn't want to like it, didn't want to feel this pull toward a woman who wasn't Abigail. Sure as sunrise, attraction for his secondhand bride was *not* part of the plan, ran counter to their agreement, and definitely not a good idea.

Nothing had changed. He *still* didn't want a wife—just a help meet. Given her abusive son-of-a-bitch husband still lived, John couldn't be more than a stand-in husband and he'd do well to remember that.

Reluctantly, he put her away from him and cleared his throat. "We'll practice again, later."

He wished he hadn't noticed the disappointment dampening her happiness. He didn't want to leave her like this, but he had to—for his own sanity, and for the safety of the family—his primary objective. "Lock up the house tight, reload and keep the rifle close at hand. I won't be gone but a short while."

She stood a little straighter, nodded. Confidence looked mighty fine on her.

Shoot.

He scrubbed a paw over his face, fighting the urge to kiss her brow in parting. "I'll ride to Gustav Larson's to borrow a watchdog."

AS IT TURNED OUT, John was gone less than an hour.

Millie found herself fairly melting with relief when he rode back into the dooryard, a black and white dog trotting at the horse's flank. The canine looked mean, one blue eye and one brown. A pink tongue lolled as he panted. The critter made its way right to the trough and drank heartily.

John dismounted, so strong and sure of himself.

She wanted to lean on that confidence. She was loath to admit she'd watched out the window most of the time John had been away. She'd set up the ironing board near the stove and lone window where she could see out. The ironing was done but even that repetitious work did little to calm her nerves.

From where she stood, the rifle waited within easy reach. Pouches containing cartridges and caps rested on the same shelf. The weapon didn't provide as much assurance as she'd hoped.

But now John was home, and already her anxiety lessened.

He brought a packet out of his saddlebags and carried it to the porch. The contents clanked heavily on the floor boards. "Give me ten minutes to see Thunder settled, and I'll be right back."

Millie noticed he scanned the yard, looking for signs of trouble. So he wasn't so at ease as she'd assumed. For the first time, she noted a holster strapped to his leg and the butt of a pistol peeking from it. He'd ridden armed. Good.

She returned to supper preparations, lifting the pot of beans she'd had soaking to the hottest part of the stove, then gathered ingredients for a batch of cookies. She punched down the bread dough she'd left to rise. Just as she covered the bowl with a tea towel, she heard John's familiar footfalls on the porch.

He'd brought tools from the barn and set to work hanging a heavy wrought iron triangle from the porch eave by a sturdy chain. He wielded the hammer, pounding a nail. His shoulders bunched with the effort. In profile he seemed more resolute than usual.

She knew what the triangle was for.

Gratitude filled her, near to overflowing. It seemed she continually owed him more and more. She still couldn't believe he hadn't turned her out upon hearing the truth.

John. Her protector.

Inside, young Oliver chattered away with Benjamin. She ought to check on the little boys, but kept her attention on John. He seemed so sure of himself. So capable. He affixed an iron bar, dangling on long chain.

"Anyone asleep?" he asked.

Thoughtful, too, and considerate of his children's need for sleep. What a good pa.

"No. They're all awake."

He tested it, beating the device forcefully. The iron's clatter resonated, no doubt carrying far and wide.

He smiled, the pleasure of it reaching his eyes. "So you can call me when I'm out in the fields. Something goes wrong and you need me quick, you ring this triangle. I'll come running."

He gathered up his tools and headed back to the barn with them. Millie ought to thank him for his thoughtfulness, but words wouldn't push past the lump in her throat. She hadn't felt this much concern from anyone else, even from Oliver—though he should have made her feel this cared for—since before the war. She'd been on her own, with no one to turn to for help, for *so* long.

He made her feel...*valued*.

Shooting lessons, the watchdog, an iron triangle, putting their safety ahead of planting. Every bit of it proclaimed he cared. About *her*.

More and more, John proved to be everything she wished Oliver had been.

John headed back across the dooryard, chickens scattering before his boots. The dog had caught a scent and began circling the house, inherently grasping his duty.

Sunlight caught on John's brown hair, shining with highlights of red-gold fire. He'd head out to the fields now. Of course he would. The planting had to be done, and soon. He'd mentioned the urgency just days ago and the work wasn't completed. He'd lost a good week of prime planting when Abigail had died, seeing to the burial, the children's needs, getting letters off to her relatives back east. And contracting with the Agency.

He stepped onto the porch, the floor boards creaking beneath his weight. She smiled at him, hoping the gesture seemed genuine. If he needed to plant, she would let him go without complaint.

He'd armed her with a weapon and a dog to warn her of approaching danger. He'd provided a means of calling to him, even miles away. It *would* be all right if he returned to work. She forced a smile, one she hope spoke of acceptance.

His big, warm hand cupped her elbow. His gaze snagged hers and held. "Today I'll work close to home, keep an eye on you and the children."

WHILE THE CHILDREN NAPPED in the bedroom, Millie sat with a basket of mending. All John's work shirts required repair and the children's clothes needed hems let down. Once the mending was caught up, she'd start sewing new items from the fabric he'd provided.

She was surprised when John met a rider in the dooryard and brought him in.

"Gustav Larson, meet my wife, Mrs. Permilia Gideon."

"Missus." Larson, a raw-boned man, stood inches taller than John.

"Mr. Larson," Millie said, dipping a curtsy. "I'm pleased to meet you."

"Ya. And you." The Swede's accent resonated heavily. "My dog keep you plenty safe. Good dog."

"Thank you." Something about the neighbor's demeanor made Millie immediately comfortable with him. How could she not be, with John at home?

"We'll get to work," John said. "Sorry, Mil. The noise will probably keep the children awake but it can't be helped."

John's simple courtesies still caught Millie off guard. It never would've occurred to Oliver to remember their babe—he'd raised a ruckus whenever he wanted to. "I don't mind. You do do what you need to."

Curious, she watched the men carry in tools from the barn and Larson's saddlebags. John set down a box of window panes he must have had tucked away.

Ah, so that's what this work project would be. A window. Set into the north-facing wall—her previously blind side.

Emotion overtook Millie, as strong and unsettling as a northern wind. John's protectiveness, his preparations for the worst possible scenario had her feeling tender affection for him.

It would never do.

He wouldn't love her, and he'd made it clear he didn't want her to love him. They'd struck a bargain.

But watching him take an ax to the sturdy north wall of his home, cutting away the solid logs until a hole large enough for a two-man saw could be managed, she had a hard time remembering her vow.

Her tender affections were getting out of control.

The men thrust the two-man saw forward and back, with Larson outside and John inside. Sweat ran down John's face and he mopped at it with his rolled shirtsleeve. John's sweat-dampened shirt stuck to his well-muscled chest. Cords of muscle and tendon stood out on his arms.

This tremendous effort to install a new window made her realize she teetered on the edge of falling in love with her not-quite husband.

Only because he's kind, thoughtful, protective. Accepting.

Throwing his shoulder into additional work, and doing it gladly.

Because of me.

For me.

She truly liked what his actions told her: he cared, he wanted her safe, he would provide. His touches, so gentle and kind, said he'd come to care for her as a person, a human being.

Everything she'd prayed Oliver would be…everything she wanted and more than she needed.

John Gideon may never love her, Millie knew, but she feared it was too late for her battered heart.

She had fallen in love with him.

Chapter Six

THE NEXT SEVERAL DAYS passed quietly. John kept himself occupied near the house with odd jobs, saying the planting could wait, that his family's safety was his top priority. Millie did her best to avoid thoughts of Oliver's looming threat and the most unsettling realization that John had come to mean *everything* to her.

Since the letter had arrived, she hadn't been able to sleep soundly. She heard every creaking board of this house, every dance of the wind through the trees. She often heard John turn over on his pallet bed in the other room and doubted he'd slept well either.

She'd taken to leaving the bedroom door open several inches, just so she could hear him breathe. She needed to know he was near.

Early the morning of wash day, she gathered all of the soiled clothing and bedding and set about heating water.

The two little ones were back to bed for a nap, while Oliver and Benjamin built a tower of blocks. John fixed the corral's fence. The dog trotted from one corner of the barn to the rear of the house, his tail wagging.

Even as anticipation of Oliver's strike built to an overwhelming pitch, she had begun to wonder if it would all come to naught.

Millie knew every dime would go to keeping him in

drink, and he hadn't had steady employment in more than a year. It seemed most unlikely he'd have the wherewithal to pay train fare. Maybe he wouldn't do a thing about knowing where his wife and son had gone.

She scrubbed the babies' dresses against the washboard and wrung them out. The boys' trousers came next. As she worked her way through the diminishing pile of dirty clothes, her mind wandered to John, as it seemed wont to do.

He never failed to appreciate her cooking, her care of the children—just this morning he'd shown such joy over baby Sarah's growth. He'd deemed her milk of the finest quality, given the new chubbiness of Sarah's arms and legs.

His appreciation warmed her clear through.

His appreciation would be enough—she would *make* it be enough.

She dunked her two dresses into the washtub next. The one she now wore had been Abigail's—too long at the ankle, rolled up several times at the wrist, and the waist rode several inches low, but it had lots of wear left in it. She couldn't let a serviceable dress go to waste. Wearing it let her launder her own. Later, she'd remake it to fit better.

Most of the clothing she washed had worn thin, already patched at the elbows and knees. Soon, she vowed, she'd find time to sew trousers and coats for the boys. They'd need them before long.

John's clothes muddied the wash water, some little better than rags. He could use replacements before next season. Somewhere, midst the care of four little ones, she simply had to find time to sew.

She wanted to please John, more, with every passing day. She sighed heavily. It was proof just how hard she'd fallen for him.

She had exchanged the wash water twice by the time she reached the last of her laundry pile—the rags. Her hands were chapped and reddened from the harsh lye soap, but that couldn't detract from the sense of satisfaction she felt from a job well done.

Glancing over the basket of wet laundry awaiting a rinse, she mentally cataloged every bit of clothing, bed sheets, and cloths in the household. She didn't want to leave anything unwashed. Now that she was on a schedule, she wanted to keep this chore to just one day a week, if possible.

Yes, she'd gathered all the cloths used for dishes, all the bedding and nappies. All of John's shirts and trousers, his underclothing and socks. Though her mind had wandered, she remembered washing her pantalets, chemises, petticoats, aprons, and bonnets. Both tattered dresses.

And the rags used for cleaning. Yes, that should account for everything.

The laundry tub was far too heavy for her to pour out alone, so she had just immersed two buckets into its depths to partially empty it when John came around the corner of the house.

"Let me." He hurried to the porch, picked up the filled washtub with ease, and carried it to the empty corner of the kitchen garden to pour out.

"Thank you."

"Happy to be of service." His smile seemed so warm, so familiar. He set the tub back on the porch. "More hot? Or ready for cold water?"

"Cold. But I'll draw it. You go back to whatever you were doing."

"I got this." He carried the empty washtub to the well and spun the handle to lower the bucket. In quick succession he drew water, poured it into the tub, and lowered the pail again.

Millie watched the play of muscles in John's shoulders and arms—such an extraordinary specimen of male vitality—and caught herself staring just moments before he bent to heft the tub. She cleared her throat, averted her gaze, and turned her flushed cheeks away from him. One glance, and he'd know...that she'd been ogling or that she'd fallen for him—and neither pleased her.

"Thank you. Much obliged." She took her seat on the stool and gathered the first pieces of laundry to rinse.

His hand squeezed her shoulder, so gentle. And welcome. His touch seemed to linger, sending her heartbeat into an erratic dance.

"Anytime. When I'm home, you should let me lift that. Call me when you're done rinsing, and I'll dump it."

"I will." She swished the tablecloth and aprons vigorously so she wouldn't have to look at him.

"O.K." He chuckled softly.

"What?" She glanced up, met his gaze.

"Something wrong, wife?"

She appreciated his decision to stick close to home, to protect the family, but at this moment, she wasn't managing his nearness well. "No."

Why her mind chose that instant to suddenly alight on the stack of clean cloths still tucked in her sack, she couldn't say—the rags she used during her monthlies to spare her undergarments.

The rags she hadn't needed since arriving in Kansas.

Her heart rolled over, slow but sure. She found herself quickly counting back, trying to remember how long it had been. *When* had her last courses come?

His gaze still searched her face—he must've taken note of the color draining from her face. "You feeling all right?"

"Yes. I am well."

He paused a beat, as if he didn't believe her. "I'm hungry for a bite to eat. How 'bout you leave that chore for a few minutes and join me?" He smiled in that gentle way of his. "I'd like to visit with you 'bout something I've been thinking on."

She nodded, shoving the unwanted, horrible thoughts away until she could be alone. John had already gathered the boys, one on each arm and carried them inside. She followed them into the kitchen, but try as she might, her mind wouldn't quit worrying the idea now that it had taken root.

She'd left Oliver three weeks ago, or so, and been here with John just over two weeks. True to their agreement, John hadn't touched her, not like that.

But Oliver had, not that long ago.

It had been easier for her to submit than risk his ire by refusing him. He'd been corned on rotgut and in a foul mood. There had been no tenderness nor love in the act.

Oliver's degrading words had cut her to the quick that night. She'd forget the whole thing, if she could.

Maybe her lack of courses was simply the worry, the anxiety that had driven her to leave Oliver. Or maybe the malnourished last many months with him and caused her to skip?

While she washed her hands and those of their sons, John sliced yesterday's bread and brought out butter and jam. Their midday meals had become simple and required very little work on her part. She found she appreciated John in these little things as much as she did in the grand gestures.

He heard Margaret wake and brought her out, evidently in a dry nappy and dress—Oliver had never changed a diaper. John seated his daughter then washed his hands.

"I've been thinking of adding on to the house," John commented, as he tore bread pieces small enough for little Margaret to feed herself. "Once I get the last of the winter wheat drilled, it would be a good time to start building."

Was she just one month gone? Two?

John paused and searched her face.

She tried to smile and nodded. "Yes."

"We'd benefit from another bedroom. One for you and the girls." He spread jam on his own slice of bread, hesitant, it seemed, to look at her. "One for me and the boys."

Her thoughts headed straight back to her quandary. That awful last time with Oliver, it had been unbearably hot, a spell that had lasted a full week of uncommonly high temperatures. Had it been July or August?

She'd always been regular, except for a handful of months after young Oliver's birth—she'd skipped several months then. She recalled her courses in July, over Independence Day, and perhaps August. But September?

John poured another few swallows of milk in each boy's cup. "The worst of winter won't set in until December, and snows here are mild. I see it as a needful expense, but could wait if you prefer we put the funds elsewhere."

Startled, she engaged fully in his comments. "Are you asking my opinion?" The idea caught her completely unprepared.

Oliver had never so much as informed her of his spending. He'd bought her a beautiful wedding ring, given her the grand gift of a quick wedding trip to Philadelphia with two nights in a beautiful hotel. What an absurd waste of money, given the poverty they'd sunk to.

Never once had Oliver discussed money with her, much less asked for her thoughts on financial matters. Not when times were good and not when times were bad.

She didn't want to think about Oliver any more. She hoped and prayed he'd never come, that the precautions John and she had taken would prove unnecessary. Perhaps she really would be safe here, and so would John.

"Yeah," John said, laughter lurking in his playful tone, "I am. You seem surprised."

"An additional bedroom sounds wonderful." She tried to smile. But deep in the back of her mind she couldn't let the nagging feeling pass. With child? Was it possible? She didn't want it to be.

Not with her hands so full with four little ones under age three, and now that she'd fallen in love with John, she didn't want to carry anyone else's babe.

What would John say? The mere thought raised her anxiety. Oliver would not have been happy; he hadn't been pleased to hear she was with child when his son was to be born. With that only experience behind her, she had to wonder if John would be upset he had yet one more mouth to feed.

"Millie?" He covered her hand with his.

Belatedly, she realized he and the boys had finished eating and her bread sat before her, untouched.

"Yes?"

"You don't sound happy about my plan to add on to the cabin." His smile dimmed and he held her gaze for a long moment. "Don't you want to talk about it?"

"I'm just surprised. You might be accustomed to asking your wife for input, but Oliv—" She cleared her throat, finding speaking of him distasteful. "He never asked my opinion, never discussed money with me."

"That's a shame." John took a wet cloth to Benjamin's sticky fingers. "Two heads are nearly always better than one."

Her thoughts had already drifted back to pick at the dread gathering around the question of her monthlies. She hated the thought of waiting weeks or even months to know for sure.

"You're distracted." He swept a thumb over her cheek, dragging a lock of escaped hair to the side. "Don't worry."

She tried to nod.

"We're ready. If he comes, we'll stand together."

His touch to her jaw and cheek felt so good.

He withdrew, too soon. "Eat," he urged. He cleared away the table. "No more laundry until you've eaten."

"Who's tired?" he asked of Oliver and Benjamin, bouncing them on his muscled arms.

"No!" Benjamin fought the idea of naps. He'd taken to napping as little as possible. "Mama!" He twisted on his father's arm, reached for Millie.

"Oh, no you don't," John soothed. "Let Mama eat."

He carried the two toward the bedroom. Margaret sat at the table, still sucking on bites of bread and jam.

How easily John had taken to calling her mama. In Abigail's place.

Abigail. The woman who'd sat at this table with John, who'd lived in this house, cooked his meals and shared his bed. The woman he'd included in decision making, whom he'd provided for and loved with all of his heart.

What a very big heart John had.

Would there ever be room enough for her in his heart?

She forced herself to eat her bread and jam, drink the milk he'd poured for her. But her mind wouldn't stop churning on the evidence.

All she knew about John's first wife was that she'd died when their youngest, Sarah, was ten days old. Had it been a fever? Consumption? Complications of childbirth? Millie didn't know. John had only mentioned that Abigail had been weakened.

The timing seemed suspicious; Abigail may well have died from a difficult birthing. She couldn't help but wonder how John would feel if faced with yet another wife facing childbirth. He might not be ready.

She quickly gathered the lunch dishes, poured hot water over them, and cut a few shavings of soap into the water. She scrubbed one plate, then two.

Her chest tightened. So did her hands on the dishrag and knife.

John had alluded to his reasons for wanting a marriage

in name only. Part of it had been his grief over losing a beloved wife so recently; he wasn't ready to replace Abigail in his heart nor in his bed. But Millie suspected that wasn't the whole of John's reasoning.

He'd said Abigail had perished as a result of too many babies, too close together. Could very well be he'd chosen to keep Millie at arm's length to prevent this very outcome. After all, she'd seen men remarry quickly after the death of a wife, and their marriages may not have been love matches, but they were marriages in every sense of the word, evidenced by the new wife bearing a child near their first anniversary.

No sense revealing her suspicions to her husband. After all, she didn't know for sure. She *couldn't* be sure. She's missed only one or two monthlies and that could be easily explained away.

Why add to his burden now?

If it were true, when she knew for certain, she would tell him. But not until.

JOHN SAT AT DAVID FARNHAM'S HEARTH that Sunday afternoon, his belly comfortably full and baby Sarah asleep in his arms. Farnhams' cabin held the lingering aromas of roasted ham, boiled potatoes, yeast rolls, and mingling spices in buttery sweets.

Peaceful as the day was, one could almost forget the ever-present threat of Millie's good-for-nothing *former* husband. From the looks of things, Millie's constant worry had been left behind as the wagon rolled down the road to Farnhams'.

Good. She needed a rest from it all, and it pleased John he could give her this respite.

But that didn't mean he could forget the troubles altogether. This far from town, a man had to rely on his neighbors.

David's youngest, a boy of four years, wiggled off his papa's lap and scampered back to the bedrooms where the children played.

Outside, wind gusted fallen leaves and twigs past the

window. John met David's gaze.

"What is it?" David asked.

"I need you to make a trip into town, tomorrow, if possible." John passed over the letter Millie had addressed to Clara. "This needs to make the post."

David read the address, nodded slowly. "Everything O.K.?"

John glanced toward the women, chatting quietly as they washed and dried dishes, paying the men no mind.

"Millie's worried about a friend back home, and she well should be." John had thought this all through, determined no one need know Millie's circumstances, not the circuit judge, not the gossips of Abilene, and not his closest neighbors and friends. John would keep her confidences.

"There's more. We have reason to believe a troublesome man intends to follow Millie here. To us."

David whistled low, the sound he typically made when surprised by a bit of news. He gestured to the pistol holstered at John's thigh. "I wondered 'bout that."

He'd stay armed and ready, as long as it took. "Just a warning to keep your eyes open. Can't say when or if this fellow will show his face, of if he'll mistake your place for mine."

"Who is this guy? What does he want?"

"A ne'er-do-well who doesn't want to see Millie happy, and doesn't want to see her with me." That's all he'd say about that.

"I see why you're sending me to town. You need to stick close to home and your missus."

"Yeah."

"I believe I'll take the whole family with me into Abilene tomorrow. Need anything while I'm there?"

He and Millie had gone over the stores that morning, in anticipation of this opportunity. It might be weeks before he'd dare leave her alone to take his turn heading to Abilene for supplies. He pulled money and their grocery list written on a scrap of paper from his pocket, offering both to David. "Thanks, friend. I'll get square with you when all this is over."

David nodded. "I'll see to it you will." Leave it to David

to make light at a time like this.

John found his attention turned to Millie. Heat from the wash water had reddened her hands. She'd pushed her dress sleeves up to her elbows, revealing too-thin forearms and skin pale from lack of sunlight. But her figure was filling out. She'd regained some curve to her profile and the better of her two threadbare and oft-patched dresses fit more naturally.

Just looking at Millie so enjoying the association of another woman made John realize it could get mighty lonely with only babies for company.

She hadn't complained, not once.

To look at her now, enjoying washing dishes with her new friend, it was clear she needed this reprieve as much as he did. Perhaps more. And not just from the constant fear of what Oliver would do—but from the everyday drudgery of motherhood. Grace had taken to Millie quickly, welcoming her into her home and her confidence.

Millie needed adult companionship. Why he hadn't realized this before, he couldn't say, but vowed to spend more time just talking with her.

He could do that. He *should* do that.

He would do more to make friends with Millie. She was too good a woman to risk losing to loneliness.

After all she'd done for his babies, after taking as much of a chance on him as he'd taken on her, it only seemed the decent thing to do.

Husband in name only didn't change the fact he was her husband.

David must've noted John's attention riveted on the women because he leaned closer. "Our wives have taken to each other like a bee to a blossom. This is good for them."

"Bring the family to our place next Sunday." It'd be something for Millie to look forward to. Maybe take her mind off the present troubles. He'd help carry the burden of the extra work the company would cause.

"Mother," David addressed his wife, "Sunday dinner at the Gideons' next week?"

The women's smiling gazes sought one another for the briefest of moments. Grace chuckled. Millie looped her arm through her friend's.

"Yes," Grace answered, her face lit with joy. "Definitely yes."

"You up for that, Mrs. Gideon?" John liked the easy smile on Millie's lips. Seemed the woman became more and more appealing with every passing day.

"David," Grace called, indicating the dish pan.

He was quick to do his wife's bidding and carry the wash water out. A blast of much cooler air swirled inside when the door opened. Grace shut it behind him.

Childish laughter filled the large cabin. David and Grace had six children, their older ones happily entertaining the young'uns.

In John's arms, his baby stirred, waking from her nap and fussing. He did his best to soothe Sarah. She wasn't accustomed to so much noise.

Grace took a plate of molasses cookies to the children, returned and cut wedges of pumpkin pie for the adults. John's mouth watered in appreciation of Grace's fine baking. Sarah's fussing increased so he put her to his shoulder as Millie took her seat beside him and nibbled a taste of pumpkin filling.

"Thank you, ma'am." John accepted a slice of pie, topped with sweet whipped cream. He set his plate on a small table at his elbow and managed to get a forkful to his mouth without spilling it. "Delicious."

"You flatter me unnecessarily. A second piece is already yours."

"Promise?"

Grace waved away his teasing and settled next to David with their dessert plates. Millie set hers aside and stood to gather the baby.

He handed Sarah over. Millie would know what to do.

She murmured comforting, soothing nonsensical words to Sarah, then, "Mama loves you, Sarah. You're hungry, aren't you? I'll feed you, Sweetie."

Before he could help himself, his heart warmed with appreciation—and something a lot like affection—for this dear woman, his wife.

Millie turned to Grace. "May I nurse our daughter in your bedroom?"

"Certainly." Grace showed Millie through the bedroom

door for privacy.

Grace had barely returned to the main room when Millie's words struck him. *Our daughter. Mama loves you.*

Contentment—the only label he could put on the comforting sensation rolling through him. Millie took to the children right fine. And his little ones loved her. Abby would have approved of Millie.

"You've got yourself a good woman, there." David scraped his fork across his plate to gather crumbs and last of the cream.

Grace went to the back of the house to check on the children.

"That I do." A twinge of something too much like guilt, too much like gratitude he didn't deserve, twisted inside him. He hid it by tucking into his pie. Rich pumpkin custard was his favorite sweet.

"Have to admit, friend," David spoke low, as to not be overheard, "when you spoke of writing away for a woman, I thought it wouldn't end well."

"It's not ended, not yet." Their lives together had just begun. There was still so much to learn about her, so much opportunity stretching forward. He hadn't anticipated actually liking or appreciating a help meet, much less this growing affection for her.

Almost as if he'd done something very wrong, guilt tugged at his conscience. He wasn't supposed to *care for* Millie, not like this. Abby would've understood friendship, working alongside one another, but these tender feelings of affection, man for a woman, bordered on betrayal.

He didn't want to think about his growing ardor for Millie, so he tucked the thoughts away, and focused on the conversation and pastry melting on his tongue.

David chuckled. "No. Not yet." He fell quiet for a moment, his thumb and forefinger smoothing his beard thoughtfully. "I hope it don't end for a good long while."

"Amen to that."

"Luck of the draw being what it was," David commented after a pause, "you did mighty fine for yourself."

Grace rejoined the men, and John found himself falling into silence while he enjoyed his second piece of pie. *Yes. Millie was something special.* He'd found it easy to allow her to replace Abigail in his home, as the mother of his children. Millie, with her over-sized capacity to love his motherless children had crept into his heart.

How had he become so fond—too fond—of his new wife?

Not what he'd planned to do and not what should have happened.

Grace set her fork on her dessert plate. "I like her."

His thoughts, exactly. In fact, he liked Millie a mite too much.

Of this, he believed, Abigail would definitely *not* approve.

John's eyes drifted shut as loneliness tiptoed in, as she so often did, bringing whispered memories of sunlight glinting on Abigail's golden curls, the melody of her laughter that had so easily captured his youthful heart. How he loved her, still.

With his one great love buried so recently, *why* had his traitorous heart so much as *noticed* another? Love for Abby had filled his heart so completely, there shouldn't be room for anyone else.

A better man wouldn't find himself drawn to another.

Oblivious to John's turmoil, Grace and David continued the conversation, praising Millie's love for the children. Seemed they'd been watching her closely this day.

In the back bedroom, childish laughter turned to tears. One of the little ones wailed. It wasn't long and his own toddler, Margaret, came running, her little shoes tapping a pitter-patter on the floorboards.

"Mama!" Margaret wailed, her small fists swiping away tears from plump cheeks. "Mama?"

John shoved aside his inner turmoil and reached for his daughter. "Come here, Sis."

"No!" Margaret's gaze turned away, searching for Millie. Near the stove, amongst the adults, at the table. Incoherent sobs and sadness welled in his little girl.

His children were so young, they'd already forgotten the fair-haired mother who'd been lost. The ease with which Margaret replaced Abigail with Millie brought a melancholy sadness to bear within John.

He'd brought Millie here to take over that vacancy, to

fill the role of mother. Wasn't this what he'd planned, he'd banked on? Finding a compassionate, loving woman to mother his motherless children? Hadn't he planned for Millie to love them, and they to love her in return?

Was he wrong to let this happen?

A pang of grief for his lost wife clenched its talons about his aching heart. To hide the unwelcome emotion, he stood and swept Margaret into his arms. "Hey, Sis. Don't cry."

"Mama!"

The bedroom door opened, revealing Millie's concern. "John, she can snuggle with us."

Margaret squirmed in his arms, fighting to be put down. Instead, he carried her to the doorway where Millie stood, modestly tucked behind the door.

She met his gaze, concern and love so easily read there. He swallowed hard.

It was easier to glance down, set Margaret on her feet and allow her to squeeze through the door's narrow passage and into the room where she clung to Millie's skirts.

His gaze wandered, against his will, to his baby snuggled in Millie's arms, at Millie's breast.

Mothering his needy daughters. Nourishing and loving and caring.

Millie *was* their mama. Their new, if replacement, mother. Would it be so very wrong to allow Millie to fully replace Abigail?

For him, too?

"We'll be all right," Millie said, her voice low. She held his gaze, apparently reading too much in his eyes. Her free hand lowered to Margaret's blond curls. "Go back to your pie."

Margaret sniffed loudly, apparently wiping her nose on Millie's skirts. "Mama, Mama."

"Yes, sweet girl?"

Margaret sighed. Contented. Millie's love was all the little one needed.

He met his wife's gaze once more, a question lingering in his own empty heart. He'd sworn he wouldn't love her, wouldn't allow her to replace Abigail in his affections. But it sure felt like he'd headed that way without noticing and it seemed brutally wrong.

"I love you, Miss Margaret," Millie murmured as her gaze lowered to his little girl. She glanced up then and their gazes held.

He fancied a bit of affection directed at him, too. Or maybe that was simply his traitorous heart's desire.

Millie blinked and slowly closing the door.

John stood riveted, allowing the sight of his wife and daughters to register with full force before the latch clicked shut.

He scrubbed a hand down his face.

He was in a good deal of trouble. A man was only as good as his word, and he'd sworn to himself and to Abigail's memory that the second wife would be in name only. He'd vowed he wouldn't love Millie.

He didn't need another wife, not in the literal sense, as he already had one—Abigail, whom he would *not* forget. He sure as shootin' didn't deserve another wife, either. Not after he'd run the life out of the first one.

He'd do well to remember.

Chapter Seven

JOHN KISSED MILLIE'S FOREHEAD in farewell.

Days had passed by, falling into an easy routine between Millie and himself. He'd worked out in the field, planting the last of the crop while the weather held, and nothing had happened. She'd gotten started on clothes for the whole family, making impressive progress, and she'd been just fine at home alone.

Nervous, perhaps, but they'd discussed it at length and both had started to think any threat from Oliver had passed. It felt good to see her shooting targets like an old hand and feeling safer in her own home.

She'd even had time to hem a new gingham tablecloth for their Sunday dinner party with Farnhams coming up in a couple days. It seemed Millie had transferred much of her anxiety over Oliver to happy anticipation of their Sunday guests.

He decided to make a regular habit of Sunday get-togethers. His wife needed it, and that was reason enough for him.

"I'll be back in a couple hours to check on you," he promised, slipping his arms into his coat. The late autumn air had a decided nip to it this morning.

"We'll be fine." She seemed to stand taller, as if reassuring herself as much as him.

"I know." He smiled at this strong woman. Baby Sarah's cheeks were fat, her growth evident every time he held her. The house was spotless, every window pane cleanly reflected lamplight this predawn morning. Every pot was washed and in its place. His children had never been so well cared for, so loved.

He pushed aside the disloyal thoughts of Abigail. After all, she'd done her best, and the fault lay with him. The doctor had confirmed it.

"I'll still be back in a few hours. Dinnertime at the latest. How 'bout we take the kids and our meal and eat outside in the sunshine?" She'd begun to look so sallow. She needed more air and sunlight before winter set in. Too much of her work had kept her indoors.

"That sounds nice," she said, but wouldn't meet his gaze.

"Are you unwell?"

She paused, as if hesitating to answer his simple question. "Just tired."

Was she keeping something from him? Never one to complain, she could be coming down with something, feeling mighty poorly, and he doubted she'd tell him. "You need more sleep."

"I'm getting enough."

It seemed as if the poor woman believed she had to perform at her very best in order to please him—a hallmark of the damage Oliver had done. John vowed to do better in assuring her until she fully accepted his words as truth. "You're doing a wonderful job with the children, Millie. This house has never been so clean. As long as the little ones are cared for and we have something to eat, that's all I ask."

After a moment she nodded, as if the pause in conversation had made her aware he awaited a response. Had she heard him? He took her slight shoulders in his hands, felt the pull to draw her close.

He couldn't. Touching her like this, no matter how much he wanted to, wasn't helping him keep the affection from taking root, growing out of control. She was his wife, true, but he had solid reasons for wanting to keep their marriage a business arrangement.

Hadn't he?

She sighed. A deep, tremulous puff of air that left her deflated.

"Millie—you can talk to me. What's troubling you?" He felt helpless. "Is it Oliver?"

He found his hand at her cheek, the smooth flesh beneath his rough fingers so warm and appealing. How had he touched her so casually? He should pull away for his own good, but too soon she turned her face into his palm.

"No." Her voice was barely above a whisper. "I'm fine." She met his gaze then, worry lingering there. If not concerned about Oliver Owens, then what?

Dread tightened about his chest. Problem was, he cared—too much. Her concerns, her needs, her feelings—they all mattered to him. *She* mattered to him...more with every passing day.

He chastised himself for forgetting the vow he'd made. He would *not* love this wife. He couldn't.

He'd have to find a better way to balance his determination to be a better companion for her, to talk with her more often, and the self-preservation of keeping an emotional distance. Was it possible to do both?

Though he ached to pull her close, just for comfort and reassurance, he stepped away. "I'll be back by noon," he promised. "Please, go back to bed. You need to catch up on your rest."

She nodded, though he doubted she'd do as he asked.

Her gaze met his for just a moment before it skittered away. Though she'd denied anything was wrong, he knew better.

As he let himself out the front door, he knew two things: it was probable Oliver's threat still had her worried, more than she'd admit aloud, and he *would* be back soon to look in on her. Maybe, if he worked straight through until noon, he'd be done with that north field and could spend the rest of the day with her.

Yes. That's precisely what he'd do.

THE SUN WAS ALMOST STRAIGHT OVERHEAD when Millie heard boots on the porch stairs.

She smiled.

John was home.

How long had it been since smiles had come to her so easily? This distraction from her worries—uncertainty over Oliver, every day that passed without her courses—would be just the thing.

"Children," she called to the boys, playing with building blocks by the hearth. "Let's get your coats on."

She didn't want to waste a single moment of John's time away from the fields. She had everything ready for their picnic. The children were dressed, their shoes buttoned up, their meal packed in a basket. She knew they wouldn't go far. Perhaps just to the sun-warmed prairie grasses near the house.

Just to spend time with John put a bounce in her step.

The door opened then, and Millie turned to greet her husband with a smile, so happy to have him home.

He stepped over the threshold, but something didn't look right about the way he moved, the grasp of his hand on the door.

Recognition flashed—*Oliver!* Millie froze mid-step, all pleasurable anticipation fleeing.

Not John.

Her heart seemed to seize even as her mind raced, trying to make sense of the *wrong* husband, here, now.

Where was John? *Oh, God!* Please, no—had Oliver hurt him?

Oliver loomed in the doorway, fury marring his once-handsome features. His eyes, bloodshot from drink, squinted in the relative dimness of the home's interior and zeroed in on her.

Millie's couldn't move. Couldn't speak.

As Oliver slammed the door behind himself, all Millie could think was *why hadn't the dog alerted her?* Why wasn't it barking *now*?

Panic had her leaden feet trembling beneath her. She found herself moving in short, unsure steps to put herself between Oliver and the helpless children.

She must defend her children.

"Permilia." Oliver's tone reeked of contempt. "Run off, did you? Thought I couldn't find you?"

His filthy clothing and person stank of liquor and sweat and coal. He must've found a way to sneak aboard a train and evade the conductors checking tickets.

She couldn't respond without igniting his temper like tinder. Oh, how she'd learned that lesson. She tried to swallow around the terror clogging her throat.

"Mama?" Benjamin didn't know to remain silent and avoid Oliver's attention. But young Oliver did. The poor child clung to the back of her skirts, hiding his face from his father.

Millie reached behind to grab onto Benjamin, to tuck him against herself.

"*Mama?*" Oliver laughed, the chortle ugly and mocking. "How long you been gone, *wife?* Last I knew, we only had us one brat."

Millie dared a glance toward the rifle on the bookshelf. Four long paces and she could snatch it. Oliver must've noticed her furtive glance but mistook her focus. "Think you can get to that poker? Don't try it, woman." With one step, he blocked her access.

He was so much bigger, so much stronger than she. If it were only her, she might be able to get away. Outrun him, evade, hide. But not with four small children. No way could she grab up all four of them and elude Oliver.

No way would she try.

He wasn't *that* drunk.

These four precious innocents meant too much to her.

She shook her head to indicate agreement with his demands.

Why had she so easily trusted the footsteps on the porch were John's? She should have had the rifle trained on the doorway, in ready defense of her children.

Self recrimination burned in her gut. All that preparation for naught.

With one hand smoothing each boy's head, she stood a little taller. She'd defend them with everything she had.

Oliver raised one trembling hand, pointing a harsh, blunt finger in her face. Rank body odor assaulted her senses. She fought the reflex to gag.

"You're *my* wife, and you're coming home with me." He shook as though he'd not had a drink in a while and needed liquor badly.

In this state he got even meaner than when he'd had too much.

Come to think on it, Oliver had been just plain mean since he'd come home from war. She'd run to him, thrown herself into his arms and kissed him that day, so joyful at his safe return. Disgust curdled in her belly.

No amount of love and patience and kindness had been enough. She hadn't been able to save him.

She'd been such a fool to try. And try again.

If only she'd had the courage to kill him that last night in their chilled tenement.

She eased back a step, nodding only to pacify Oliver. If she could only make it to the door...if she could somehow convince him she needed light to see by or that she was actually leaving with him, she might get to the triangle and beat on it with the intent of warning John. *If* he were unharmed, *if* he still lived, she couldn't let him walk in unaware.

It had to be close to noon.

John would be coming home any moment. *Maybe.*

Please, God, let John be alive.

Oliver, in a mockery of gallantry, opened the front door for her. He must have noted her progress in that direction. "Ready to go so soon?" he laughed, the sound ugly.

Just five steps to the door. Three more to the triangle. She had to get there.

Two little boys clung to her skirts, hampering her movement.

She heard the unmistakable sound of a pistol's hammer drawing back. Her whole body washed hot, followed quickly by a savage chill. Oliver's pistol, in his grip. Why hadn't she assumed he'd arrived armed?

"No, no, no," Oliver chided. "Not that whelp."

"Please, Oliver—"

She didn't know why she tried reasoning with the brute. It had never worked before. With characteristic cruelty, he pulled Benjamin off Millie's skirts and shoved the boy toward the hearth. The child tumbled, knocking his head hard against the floorboards, missing the hearthstones by mere inches. Benjamin clutched his head and curled into a tight ball, his sobs wrenching Millie's heart. She wanted nothing more than to pick him up, soothe away the bumps and scrapes.

"Leave him be." Oliver shoved her toward the door. She stumbled, caught herself, and felt herself slipping into the old ways of submitting to Oliver's demands, doing anything and everything to keep him calm, to diffuse his temper.

She hated that weakness in herself. Oh, she'd play along, but she wasn't a fool. She would die before leaving this homestead with him. But she had to get to that triangle, and the triangle was outside. So through the door she went, clinging tightly to her son's hand. Oliver might shoot her in the back for ringing that triangle—but she had to attempt it. She saw no other way to save her family.

The moment she registered the empty nail where the triangle had hung only an hour before, Oliver chuckled with menace behind her. The animal toyed with her, relished her fear. Craved it.

God, she hated him.

He tapped her shoulder with the barrel of his pistol.

She spun to put their son behind and realized what Oliver held dangling from his crooked finger.

An iron paddle. "Looking for this?"

Chapter Eight

OLIVER GRABBED HER ARM, hauled her back into the house, dragging young Oliver on her skirts. His fingers dug into her tender flesh. He'd leave a bruise. But that wasn't her greatest concern. He slammed the door.

Benjamin screamed in terror.

Millie wrenched out of Oliver's hold and picked up the lad. She held him close, turning his face away from the intruder.

Oliver just laughed, that mean, feral cackle that raised fine hairs on her arms and left her cold inside.

"You really thought you could leave me?" he bellowed, threatening to strike her with the iron paddle. He took a menacing step closer, his breath putrid in Millie's face. "You're pathetic. Put that whelp down and you look at me when I talk to you."

Shaking with fright, She set the lads together with their pillow in the corner—unfortunately not the side of the hearth with her rifle, for Oliver stood there—and turned to face her former husband.

He raised the rod, threatening. "You ran off and shacked up with another man? Said your 'I do's'? That makes you a bigamist, a filthy, lying bigamist. Does he know you're already married, to *me?*"

Millie couldn't help it, she flinched. At least John

already knew the truth. "Yes. He knows."

"Oh, does he?" Oliver swung his wasting body toward the boys, pointing a long finger. "Does his whelp know you're a whore?"

She'd take all the verbal abuse in the world if she could keep his attention off the boys. He didn't give her a chance.

"You're leaving with me, *Mrs. Owens,* and you're leaving with me *now.*" He shook harder now, the withdrawals from liquor growing worse. Already volatile, he'd only get more so. He'd start swinging his fists and wouldn't stop.

There was no hope for it—she was on her own. She couldn't rely on help from John, who might not return until it was far too late, if at all. The children had no one to rely on but her.

The idea came quickly, easily. Why, of course. She'd use Oliver's weaknesses against him. It was the only way.

"Would you like a drink, Oliver? Before we go." Without taking a step, she indicated a shelf next to the hearth, near the boys. A half bottle of rotgut. Not enough to buy much reprieve, but some. She could only hope the liquor would tame his agitation just enough to diminish his rage against the children.

"You messing with me, woman?" Oliver's gaze was on the bottle, with something too much like lust in his eyes.

"I'll get it for you." No way did she want him near her sons. Up on tiptoe, she reached the bottle she'd found while dusting. "Come, have a seat," she urged in her mildest, placating tone. It had worked before.

Oliver shuffled forward, his gaze locked on the bottle. She led him away from the children, away from the bedroom door where the babies cried. Their pitiful whimpers had escalated to wails. Margaret screamed for her. His shouts and door slams had woken them.

She pulled out a chair for him, this one intentionally the furthest from her exits. Her choice put the sturdy hand-hewn table between him and her precious charges.

Oliver dropped into his seat and grabbed the bottle from her grasp. He plunked the pistol onto the tabletop and uncorked the bottle with his teeth. He sniffed the contents and put the rim to his lips. One long pull drained the bottle's meager contents halfway.

She didn't have much time.

"I'll quiet the children. They're disturbing you."

"You do that," he spat, the bottle already against his lips.

She hesitated to turn her back, knowing full well what he was capable of. But she did it. The boys huddled together in the far corner, their pillow providing a poor barrier between themselves and Oliver. Should she bring them into the bedroom with the babies? There was no exterior door, only a window. Was it possible to lower the lads outside to run and hide? With Sarah only three months old, she knew there was no way she could get all four children to safety. They were helpless.

But she could try to comfort the youngest two. Try to calm and quiet them to prevent provoking Oliver. In the bedroom, she gathered the little girls into her arms.

"Make them shut up!" Oliver threw the glass bottle against the wall. It shattered with splintering force.

The surprising sound made Sarah startle and squall again in Millie's arms, and Margaret joined in. Poor babies were terrified.

In the doorway of the bedroom, Millie could see the boys now huddled with the pillow over themselves like a blanket, hiding.

She wanted nothing more than to scoop up all four children and walk out of this house. Away from Oliver and his demands. If only she had a chance of carrying all four. If only she could carry two and trust the two small boys to keep up with her. Even inebriated, Oliver was too quick with his guns, too good a shot. She wouldn't put it past him to shoot two little boys in the back.

He'd kill his own son. She knew that to be true.

And if he'd kill his own, why not three he had no blood ties to?

John would come home and find the carnage. Blood spilled and his family massacred.

Sole responsibility lay with Millie—she had to make sure that didn't happen.

She whispered to the girls, trying to comfort their little bodies tight to her chest, urging them to silence. Her own son had learned too early to heed warnings to be quiet. These little girls didn't understand.

"Another bottle!" Oliver demanded.

There wasn't any more. At least not that she knew of. Telling him so would only invite his wrath. She had to distract him. "I have fried chicken ready. Boiled Eggs. Lemonade. Would you like a nice meal?"

Oliver stood, the force of his momentum throwing the chair onto its back. "Food? I don't want food. Get me another bottle." His voice had dropped to that deadly calm that signaled his anger would momentarily erupt.

Now the boys were crying too. Benjamin far louder than young Oliver.

She could lie to Oliver outright, tell him the stores were kept in the barn and take the children out there with her. Even if she hid the children, he'd find them in a moment; they were too noisy to hide effectively, and she had no way of impressing upon such young babes the need for silence.

She might put on a good show for Oliver about bringing a bottle back, but bring a weapon of some kind instead.

Could she pull off that kind of deception? She'd have to try.

"I'll get more, Oliver. It's in the barn, to keep cool." Holding tight to both girls, she moved to where the little boys hid. "Come with me, boys. Let's go to the barn for another bottle."

"You're lying," Oliver accused, his tone brash. The liquor had whetted his lust for more, and seemed to have thrown fuel on his anger. "You're worthless, woman. Worthless *and* a liar." How many times had she heard these vile words?

And as she stood there, unable to coax the boys out from hiding behind the useless protection of a pillow, unable to carry them all, she felt utterly worthless. She hadn't been able to protect these innocents from her own husband—even though she'd known he would come after her.

What kind of a mother did that make her?

"Don't know why I bothered to hunt you." Wildness had settled in his rheumy eyes—wildness she'd seen only a glimmer of before, the night he'd split her lip and blackened her eye with his fist, cracked her ribs. Her fear spiked, reaching new heights.

The truth of it slammed into her with more force than his fists ever had.

She'd never be free of him.

Never.

In Oliver's twisted mind, whatever his reasons, he didn't want her to know a moment's peace. He suffered, and so must she.

She should have killed him that night, when he'd been unconscious at her feet. She'd had the chance, and she'd let it pass, believing she'd made the better choice.

Resignation seeped into her weary bones, making her all but weep. To pacify him, she nodded. Hung her head in shame. Oh, the shame was real, so very real, and required no fabrication. She'd failed Oliver, who'd come home from war, wracked with demons and broken in spirit. Perhaps if she'd loved him more, he wouldn't have become the monster who threatened her now. Maybe if she'd been the woman he needed her to be, she could've helped him heal, helped him come to love his own son born to them after those long dark years of war.

Oliver watched her closely. She felt and saw his gaze take in her slumped posture, her resignation. Grunting in satisfaction, he dropped into another chair at the table. He did not pause to right the one he'd toppled. "Find me. A drink."

She nodded, helpless to win this argument. She settled the babies in the boys' laps, huddling them together for whatever comfort they could provide one another. She made a fine show of looking through the shelves where the only bottle had been waiting. She moved a wrapped bundle aside which she knew to contain fancy dishes the family didn't use day to day. Opened a pot that contained seeds for the kitchen garden. Kept looking enough to satisfy Oliver that she'd exhausted that side of the hearth's shelves.

All in hopes of reaching, finally, the rifle that waited on the opposite side of the fireplace.

FROM THE ANGLE OF THE SUN, John figured it must be noon. He'd worked hard and fast with the planting and had finished drilling the north field just in time. By looks of the skies, they had another day before it would rain.

Perfect.

Now that the work was done, he could relax and enjoy the afternoon with his family.

His family.

Including Millie.

Sounded mighty fine. An afternoon with a leisurely meal. He'd share with her his plans to add two bedrooms off the back of the house, rather than one. With the children growing, it wouldn't be long until they needed more space. He hoped the change in plans would please her.

And maybe tomorrow he'd help her pull up the remaining vegetables in the kitchen garden. Temperatures and length of the days seemed just right—they'd have a hard frost within the week.

He hoped both ideas would meet with her pleasure.

He found making her happy brought him an unwarranted amount of joy.

He couldn't help whistling a merry tune as he led the horses back into the barn. Realizing he'd forgotten to be on the lookout as he approached the house, he stuck his head back out into the bright midday sun. Scanned. Everything looked perfectly normal to him.

It wasn't until he'd scooped grain for the horses and picked up the currycomb that he realized the dog hadn't come to greet him.

In fact, he hadn't seen the dog at all.

A flash of worry trotted up his spine. Not good.

Had that dog run off? Didn't he realize *this* was home now? He'd fed that dog enough times to have won him over.

Hadn't he?

Abandoning the horses' needs, he left the barn and scanned for the dog. He'd just put two fingers to his lips to whistle for the dog when the fine hairs stood up at the back of his neck.

Danger.

He felt it just a sure as a stiff wind.

Something was *very* wrong.

One glance at the house and he couldn't quite put a finger on it, but realized something was off. Then he saw it—the triangle he'd hung for Millie to ring was missing. Gone. As if it had never been there.

His heart seemed to shudder in his chest. He grew suddenly lightheaded with fear. He reached instinctively for the Colt he'd worn for two weeks on his hip and immediately remembered he'd taken it off in the barn. It was draped over the horse's stall.

He'd just turned back inside to get that necessary weapon when he caught a whiff of blood. Pungent, heavy, metallic.

Millie? The children? Bile rose in his throat even as his eyes scanned the barn's interior, praying he wouldn't find them bled out.

He caught a glimpse of a black and white coat. The dog lay in the far recesses, its throat apparently split. *Why* hadn't he noticed when he'd come into the barn?

His stomach churned with fear he hadn't known since he realized Abigail lay dying. He'd been helpless, shackled, unable to do a thing to help.

But this time, *this time,* he'd do something.

If only it weren't too late.

TEARS WELLED IN MILLIE'S EYES. How pathetic she was. How inept. She couldn't even manage her own husband's fury, everything she did angered him—and it seemed she deserved his wrath. John would be furious, too, when he learned she'd failed to protect his children.

She'd brought this disaster upon his household.

She had.

The worthless, unloved, unwanted wife of Oliver Owens.

She never should have come here. Why had she thought she could run?

Without glancing at Oliver, she hurried to the other set

of shelves, where the rifle lay. The weapon he apparently hadn't noticed. Just in case he watched her closely, she stood on a stool and reached for two bottles on the top shelf. Bottles she knew to be empty, but she had to make this look convincing.

The rifle. Her fingers trembled as she touched the smooth wooden stock just as she heard Oliver scrape his chair back and cross the room toward the children.

A moving target, she thought in despair. *I can't hit a moving target.*

Oliver could. He'd survived years of bloody battles, carrying the very pistol he'd set on the kitchen table. If he had that weapon in his hand, she'd be shot through before she could pull back the hammer and set the cap.

One furtive glance at the table—where Oliver's pistol lay.

He'd already reached the children as she clumsily bobbled the rifle, tried to swing it around and get the business end pointed at Oliver.

Her left hand fumbled with the cap. Nearly dropped it as she shook with a mixture of rage and defiance. She fit the cap over the nipple, centering it out of habit.

She'd have one chance.

One shot.

She'd have to make it count.

Chapter Nine

THE DOG HAD BEEN DEAD for a long while, its body cold.

John fought overwhelming despair. He'd failed. *Why* had he gone to work the fields this morning? He'd seen the discomfort, the anxiety on Millie's face, and yet he'd left her.

How would he ever forgive himself?

The house was quiet. Too quiet.

Had that monster already killed his wife, his family? Had he taken them away?

John wanted to rush the house, throw open the door. He couldn't bear not knowing their fate. He had to see.

In his panic, a small flicker of caution warned him off.

What if?

If it were even possible Millie still lived, he wouldn't do her a lick of good if he stormed inside and got himself killed. He'd be of no help to them if he acted with his heart and not his head.

To hell with what he wanted. For her sake, he had to do this right.

With his Colt drawn, his jaw locked, he crept toward the house at an angle where the windows wouldn't make his approach obvious to those inside. He strained to hear any movement within the cabin. Any hint of noise.

He thought he heard a baby cry. Relief nearly swamped him, ruining his judgment. He had to be calm. Had to think.

He ran at a crouch, trying to avoid detection.

Once he reached the house he breathed deeply, leaning heavily against the solid log wall. He stooped and eased forward. Almost there.

If he could only see inside to learn what he was up against.

Slowly, he removed his hat, dropped it on the earth at his feet. With the pistol at the ready, he slowly rose to bring his eyes over the windowsill and peer inside.

THIS WAS IT.

Her only chance.

Her *last* chance.

Millie knew it just as plain as she knew she'd fallen in love with John Gideon.

If she'd ever be free, if her *children* would ever be free, she must shoot Oliver Owens dead.

She finally got the rifle into position, but shook so violently the nose of the barrel bobbed.

She stumbled down from the stool.

Oliver laughed. His cruel, jeering chuckle would haunt her the rest of her life, short though it would likely be.

Millie fought to draw a bead on Oliver's chest even as he scooped the two closest children—baby Sarah and Benjamin into his arms.

Not with love or playfulness or the kind of father-child interaction like John with his children. No. Oliver held the two innocents against his chest like a human shield.

The babies' panicked faces latched onto hers, drew her attention. Oliver's once strong arm clutched three month-old Sarah beneath one of her tiny arms but mostly about her neck. The poor baby could barely draw enough breath to cry.

Oliver, the bastard, didn't care.

He tossed back his soiled hair and scoffed. "You think you can shoot that thing?" he demanded, his tone demeaning. "I don't think so."

"Put my children down." Her voice shook, sounded pathetically weak. She cleared her throat. Demanded, "put them *down*."

"No. Don't think so. See, I figure you'll take them out when you *try* and shoot me."

Oliver clutched the babies to his chest. But his legs were exposed. She thought about drilling a bullet through his knee. That would take him down.

But would it buy enough time for her to reload?

If she missed, he'd kill her before she got to a cartridge and cap. Both were still on the shelf behind her.

Benjamin's terror-filled eyes remained locked on her face. Silent tears dribbled down his little chin. Pleaded with her for rescue. But what tormented her most was Sarah's little face rapidly darkening.

She would not allow this monster to hurt her baby.

Yes, they'd drop when Oliver released them. It was a risk she'd have to take.

His arms bunched, squeezing the babies tighter.

Their sweet faces were so close to her mark. She shook, terror like running ice water in her veins. Was she willing to risk killing her babies?

She steadied, sighted down the barrel at Oliver's ugly face. "Last chance."

WHEN JOHN CAUGHT A GLIMPSE of the drama unfolding inside his home, he experienced a whole new level of terror.

A big man, with unkempt hair, a dirty shirt and trousers—Oliver Owens, no doubt—shielded his chest with two of John's children.

And Millie—God bless her—held the Enfield on him.

She looked prepared to end his life by gunshot to the face.

But the children...

His heart in the wringer, John had barely a moment to act.

He sprinted to the back door. Into the line of fire of

Millie's rifle. At Oliver's back.

His best vantage point.

JOHN SURGED AROUND THE CORNER of the house, panic hot on his heels.

He shouldered open the back door. It crashed against the inside wall.

Everything seemed to happen in a blur, with precise focus, so slowly he noticed every bit of the excruciating scene.

Millie.

Sweet Millie. Her eyes open wide—both of them—as she took a steady aim at Oliver's face.

The door thundering open behind him must've torn Oliver's attention free, because he whirled about on the balls of his feet.

His demented gaze locked and held John's.

So this was the man who'd terrorized *his wife, and his children.*

Madness, and a fair amount of drink, from the looks of it, had turned his eyes and the bulb of his nose red.

But not as red, make that purple, as baby Sarah's face. The babe's eyes rounded wide in panic. Both little fists flailed helplessly. Her feet pumped as they dangled, finding no purchase. In that endless moment, John realized his daughter barely held onto consciousness.

The animal thought to use *his child* as a weapon against Millie.

John felt the urge to lunge at the intruder, to knock him to the ground, to wrest the children away from his manhandling grip.

In the instant before he could lunge, in the periphery of his vision, he glimpsed Millie shift the barrel from Oliver's head to his torso, seeking a larger target. She closed one eye and sighted. Oliver had turned halfway around, presenting his bare side to her, the babies out of the way, but just barely.

Millie stood less than six feet away.

From the set of her jaw and the maternal fury blazing in

her one open eye, he knew she would shoot to kill. From her target practice of late, John believed she'd hit her mark.

Realizing he stood in the line of fire, John dove aside. He slammed against the floor just as the rifle reported.

The sound of the slug piercing flesh was so near, so horrible he thought he'd never forget it. In the corner, Margaret screamed, the high piercing shriek of a little girl's horror. From the floor where he lay, John's gaze remained locked on the other man as he took a step toward Millie. Menace and fury mottled his face.

Had she missed Oliver?

Struck Benjamin instead?

A great drop of blood spattered the floor near John's face.

John scrambled to his feet, the Colt still in his grip. He had to get to his wife, had to defend her. As John found purchase, Oliver stumbled to one knee. He dropped with the force of a felled tree. One arm loosened about baby Sarah who slipped limply from his grip.

John grabbed his baby girl relieved to hear her draw an angry breath and wail. He snuggled the infant close even as he kept his pistol aimed at the other man's head.

If not yet fatally wounded, John would oblige.

No way would this monster live another day. No way would he allow him to threaten the lives of *his family*.

Millie stumbled backward, grabbed a cartridge and reloaded, quick as could be.

That same moment Oliver released Benjamin from his other arm. The boy stumbled. Sat down hard. Apparently unharmed, he scuttled away until his little back hit the rocking chair near Margaret.

John didn't dare take his gaze off the intruder. He scanned Oliver's person for weapons, seeing none. No pistol, no knife, no club.

Millie completed the reloading process and took aim at Oliver, steady and true. Her eyes narrowed at her attacker.

Oliver's bony hands clamped around the wound in his side where Millie's shot had struck home. Oliver's wheezing breaths confirmed she'd hit a lung. Blood frothed at Oliver's lips. His brows drew together with confusion.

He tottered where he perched, lost his balance and toppled to the floor.

John kept the pistol aimed at Oliver's head. With Sarah screaming in the cradle of his arm, he hurried to Millie's side, finding her gaze narrowed and pinning her former husband to the floor. Her hands were steady, her stance solid.

"Millie." Relief rushed through John, with gratitude and self-condemnation hot on its heels. He'd been too late to save her. She hadn't needed his saving.

Oliver's mouth foamed with blood. A spasm. Two. He fell motionless, his eyes glassy and unmoving.

After a long moment, Millie turned, shaking like a leafy tree in a tornado and set the Enfield back on its shelf. She threw her arms around John's middle, clutching him tightly and turned her face into the hollow of his throat. Her sobs began fully silent. Several long seconds passed before the first noise escaped her throat.

His arms full of crying woman and baby girl, John's eyes welled with tears. He couldn't help it. But kept his gaze and pistol trained on the intruder. It proved unnecessary.

Oliver lay motionless, his chest utterly still.

His Millie had freed herself from the likes of Oliver Owens.

She'd freed them all.

JOHN REMOVED OLIVER'S BODY to the shade of the cabin, outside, where Millie and the children wouldn't have to see it.

Millie bathed the children while John scrubbed the floor clean of Oliver's blood. By late afternoon, the kids had been fed and tucked into bed. It was unlikely they'd sleep through the night, but the day's horror had plumb tuckered them out. They needed healing sleep.

After dumping the bathwater, he found Millie sitting at the kitchen table, her head resting in her palms.

"Is there someone we should write?" He had to touch her, just so she knew he was there. She could lean on him.

He moved behind her and took both shoulders in his hands. "Kin of Oliver's?"

She shook her head, barely moving. "No one."

Sadness weighed upon her slight frame, seeming to wilt her remaining strength. "He lost two brothers in the war. We were all the family he had left."

He ached to touch her, hold her close, let her grieve. Folding her hands in her lap, she turned her face up to his.

Disappointment etched her features. He couldn't bear her anguish. Her pain had become his own. He opened his arms and she came to him, her embrace snug about his waist.

They stood together in the breeze of the open front door. He smoothed a hand over her back, nape to hip.

Her sigh registered more as movement than sound. "You'll notify the law?" Her voice tightened, climbed in pitch. "I'll explain, tell them everything." She must be reliving those awful last minutes, her decision to pull the trigger. "I'm *not* sorry I killed him. Will the marshal understand?"

He ached to look into her eyes, to read the emotion there, but instead held her closer and kissed her crown. "Justice hereabouts isn't what you're used to. The marshal has enough to do in Abilene proper. You did nothing wrong. He'd thank us to handle disputes on our own, defend ourselves, and not waste his time."

A long moment passed. She finally nodded against his shoulder.

It felt so good to hold her.

How had he ever believed he could deny this woman his love? She'd crept inside his heart, banishing the chill and grief and loneliness, filling him to overflowing.

A gust of wind washed along the cabin, slamming the front door he'd left open to allow the cooling breeze inside. In the bedroom, one of the boys cried in his sleep, but settled down too quickly to take Millie from him.

"I tried to love him," Millie whispered, "enough to heal him."

Sweet, compassionate Millie. He kissed her crown. How well he understood grief over what should have been.

"The man I loved before the war was charming, kind,

considerate. Full of hope and vibrancy." She sighed, the sound shaded with wistfulness. "The man who returned was damaged, a vicious drunk—and I couldn't heal him."

Yeah, he'd heard some of this before but she wasn't done. He let her talk.

"I did my best for him, at least I thought I had. Through nightmares, sleeplessness. I bit my tongue through vile cursing and fits of temper and tried to exercise patience and understanding when he lost our home and income to alcohol."

He thought that through. "There's no mending someone else, Mil."

"What is so wrong with me that he didn't want to get better? Didn't want to *be* better for me? For our son?"

She eased back then, looked him in the eye, apparently searching for answers.

He couldn't help. He didn't understand Oliver. Millie inspired John, plenty, made him want to be the best of husbands and fathers.

He took her hand in his then, so small and newly familiar within his. The connection felt wonderfully right.

Millie searched his face, evidently wanting his thoughts. Mulling it over, he found a bit of similarity in their broken dreams, past loves. "I shouldn't speak ill of the dead, especially my wife—" He scrubbed a palm down his face, blocking his sight for a moment. "Abby fell ill after Benjamin's birth—she lost weight, had no appetite, had a lump growing here," he touched his collar bone.

Millie's brows pulled together with unmistakable compassion.

"The doctor in Abilene said it was cancer. She might live for years to come, he told me, or maybe just a matter of weeks. The doc wasn't sure. But after hearing that diagnosis, Abby seemed to lose her will to fight. By then we knew she was with child again, and Margaret was on the way. I wanted her to rally, to fight for life," he swallowed, trying to steady his voice, "for our babies if not for me."

He still didn't understand how Abby could just give up, but knew the constant birthing hadn't helped any. He'd seen how the pregnancies had drained her energy, compounded the pains she suffered from that growing cancer. That blasted lump had doubled in size while she carried Sarah—and the doctor said that was to be expected, that breeding made the cancer grow at a much faster rate.

Guilt and self-recrimination lodged in his throat, making it impossible to speak without betraying the emotion.

How could he admit to this kind, compassionate woman that he'd never intended to accelerate Abby's illness? He'd only tried to love her, ease her suffering, remind her of all the good in her life. Instead, he'd gotten her with child—and hastened her death.

Millie's gentle touch on his cheek drew his gaze to hers. Sympathy and understanding, plain as day, shone in her blue eyes.

How was it that his pains with Abigail, his history, his reasons for sending for Millie to start with ended up being just what it took to understand her?

To comprehend her loss?

And made her the perfect woman to understand his?

Chapter Ten

MILLIE NEEDED AIR. Even with the door standing open, the cabin had grown stuffy, too close. She took her husband's hand, closed the door behind them to keep the heat in for the children and led him to the front porch. He sat beside her on the top step.

His shoulder leaned closer to hers. She craved his touch. Wanted nothing more than to move closer to him on that wooden step, to bring her body into contact with his from shoulder to hip to knee.

A long moment passed, both of them silent.

Thoughts tossed about in Millie's mind, a whirlwind of realizations and hopes and thoughts of the past. "Abigail's death was a tragedy. You did everything you could and it's not your fault. No one can control cancer. I know the man you are, John Gideon, and you *are* husband enough, man enough, strong enough."

He released her hand then, leaving her with immediate regret. She should have kept her own counsel.

But he put that arm about her shoulder, pulling her close, fitting her as near to the warmth of his big body as she'd desperately wanted, just moments ago. He took her hands in his. His breath brushed her temple. He inhaled, held it. His nose seemed to brush her hair, lingered there, as he pressed a kiss to her hair.

Tingles erupted at his touch, igniting a frisson from temple to toes and back again. This touch didn't feel like a mere companion, a friend.

Oh, how she wanted so much more from this husband she'd come to love.

"You're right, about the cancer, I mean—entirely outside any man's control. One thing haunts me, though. The doc said her pregnancies sped up the cancer's growth. If she hadn't been carrying—"

Millie heard the agony in his tone, the guilt he seemed to heap upon himself. She pressed a finger against his lips to silence him. "It's not your fault."

He squeezed her hand, fell silent, sighed. A moment passed in quiet reflection. "Seems to me you and I are two peas in a pod," John murmured.

"Oh?"

"If he couldn't be the man you deserved, the man he'd been before war damaged him, then it's not your doing. The war is to blame, not you."

On some level she knew he was right. It only made sense, but she was too near to the pain, the anguish of losing Oliver twice-over that she couldn't fully accept the truth. Just as her beloved John couldn't disavow responsibility for Abigail's health failing.

Two peas in a pod.

Gratitude for his perspective, his compassion warmed her clear through.

"Thank you," she breathed, grateful for the way he instilled confidence. This beloved man had proved so different from Oliver.

It was finally over.

She was free of Oliver's tyranny. Eventually, with John's help, she'd shake off the damage Oliver had done to her spirit.

JOHN DUG OLIVER'S GRAVE.

Not in the sacred plot near Abigail and their stillborn son. He couldn't bring himself to bury the man who'd tried to hurt his wife and children next to loved ones. But the burying had to happen. And one day young Oliver might want to know where his first pa had been laid to rest.

So John dug a decent hole in the shade of a Cottonwood tree a distance from the house. This lonely place would do for the likes of Oliver Owens.

He wouldn't soon forget the absolute hatred he'd glimpsed in that man's eyes moments before his death.

John's limbs shook with a combination of exertion and letdown after the crisis. Grave-digging gave a man plenty of time to sort through the jumble of thoughts in his head.

Millie. His lioness. Defending her cubs—*their* children—with such ferocity. Killing her attacker. Millie, who'd gunned down her own former husband.

In defense of *his* children.

The children who'd needed love and reassurance, who'd cried themselves to sleep and were even now tucked in their little beds in Millie's bedroom.

Sweat ran down his face. He swiped at it with a soiled shirtsleeve. Thrust the shovel blade back into the hard-packed earth.

Muscles in his arms strained. His back knotted. A cool breeze teased his sweat-soaked hair.

Millie.

She'd sobbed in his arms long enough for him to realize everything had changed.

Love for his bride welled within him, bringing with it tears he didn't want to shed.

He did *not* want to love again.

Love meant more than accepting his heart had room enough for both Abigail and Millie—it meant opening the door to having his heart crushed beneath the agony of grief. *Again.*

Losing Abigail had been more than he could bear. Loving Millie seemed ill-advised; he'd sworn he wouldn't. But his foolish heart had gone and committed again, no matter his plan.

With Oliver gone we have an honest chance at happiness.

The end of Oliver's life heralded a future without threats—a blessing for Millie and young Oliver, good for John and his three babes, and favorable for their blended family.

He hefted another shovelful as sweat burned his eyes. He paused to mop his face and neck with his handkerchief and survey his work.

And the body wrapped in a sheet.

All that remained of Oliver Owens.

John hadn't the lumber to construct a coffin and did not care.

If tables had been turned and John had been the one who died, he doubted Oliver would have given him any kind of proper burial.

This was as good as Oliver was going to get.

It was tragic, really. Tragic that war had robbed Millie of a husband she'd loved. She'd said as much, once the tears stopped flowing. On the front porch, out of sight of Oliver's corpse, Millie had clung to him and shared her regrets.

John hefted the other man into the grave. Couldn't say a prayer over him and didn't want to forgive just yet. Oliver had caused Millie far too much pain, fear, heartache.

Now that Millie was *his*, he figured he had a right to anger, at least for a while.

He shoveled dirt back into the grave until the sheet was completely covered. Kept moving earth until a mound of it was the only marker. He tamped it down firmly to keep animals away, the whole time Millie's smiling face in his mind's eye.

Sweet Millie.

Mother to his children, his *wife*.

An image of her tear-stained face, blue eyes luminous, softened with grief and love and regret.

He sighed, weary in soul as well as body.

He wanted to fight the tender feelings that tightened his throat. God help him. He'd gone and fallen, good and *gone*, for his wife.

Not what he wanted to have happen, but there it was.

One more thing outside his control.

Love meant unending pain and remorse when the inevitable loss happened.

Life was too fragile, too unsure. Yes, she was here today, but there was zero guarantee she'd be here tomorrow. A fever or pneumonia, a fall or consumption. Cancer. Could be anything.

Losing her scared him, badly.

As he headed toward home, shovel in hand, the darkness closed in around him. Peace settled, a contentment he hadn't known since before Abigail discovered that lump.

Funny thing was, the fear couldn't convince his heart to give up on the idea of loving Millie. It seemed foolish to fight it, he mused, as he made his way to the barn to clean and stow the shovel.

He'd rather be at peace and in love, accept the risk of losing her, than face endless weeks and months alone.

With a smile on his weary face, he headed toward the house.

Home, to Millie.

MILLIE SAT NEAR THE FIRE in the hearth, unable to get warm, as though ice had crept into her bones. She combed through hair still wet from her bath, listening for sounds of John returning to the house.

All four little ones were sound asleep in their beds. God willing, they'd quickly forget this horrible day.

Before John left for his odious task, he'd heated water and filled the tub. Soaking in the warmth had helped banish the chill and wash away the memories.

She left the tub for John and had more water heating on the stove to add. After digging a grave, he'd want a bath. He'd shown her such kindness, she desperately wanted to be a good wife, thoughtful, consider his needs and feelings.

It would be a simple thing to have a hot bath waiting for him.

Her heart belonged to him and it always would, in spite of his vow that he would not love her.

She had to remember his heart wasn't hers, for it still belonged to Abigail. That hurt, but she figured she could live without his love. She had his name, his kindness, protection, and friendship. He showed her familial affection—warm embraces and platonic kisses, not unlike

Gideon's Secondhand Bride

those he gave the children.

While not everything she wanted, it could be enough, would have to be enough. She reminded herself not to pine for what she could not have.

He'd already given her so much. Not just meeting her physical needs of food and shelter and safety—he'd forgiven her. He'd responded so well when she'd confided the details of her marriage to Oliver, and again when she'd revealed Oliver learned where she and the boy had gone.

Surely he would likewise respond well when she told him about the new life she suspected grew within her.

He deserved to know.

And after the day's events, this closeness they'd developed made it seem like the right time. She felt an urgency to get everything out on the table. She couldn't bear keeping anything between them.

The door opened quietly and John slipped inside. By firelight she could see the sweat-stained shirt clinging to his body. She watched him take in her nightgown, her wet hair drying in the heat of the fire. The waiting bathtub.

She went to him, drawn to his presence. "I thought you'd like to wash off the soil."

He nodded, glancing at the tub. She'd left him a clean towel and a change of clothes. Ever since her arrival, he'd slept fully dressed, because he wasn't hers.

The emotional battle of midday had brought all the old insecurities back with a vengeance, reminding her just how unprofitable a wife she'd been.

Incompetent. Untrustworthy. Worthless.

She *should* have been ready, with the rifle in hand.

Yet John's reassurances echoed in her mind. *He* believed her guiltless and had absolved her of responsibility for Oliver's long and terrible path to destruction.

He believed in her worth. That gift outweighed everything else he'd ever done for her, his forgiveness, everything. Tears stung her eyes and she averted her gaze.

How she wanted to be her *best* self, for him.

John misunderstood, bless him. "I'll, uh, get in the tub."

"Wait. I have more hot water." With a towel to protect her hand, she carried the kettle to the tub, and judging the water level low enough to accommodate the heated water, poured it in. He followed behind with the pot of steaming water.

She turned her back, carried the kettle and pot back to the stove to give him the privacy he needed to undress. She doused the lamp, the firelight more than adequate. Behind her, she heard him step into the water and sit. She made her way toward the closed bedroom door. "Goodnight, John."

"Millie..."

She paused. Hearing her name in his deep velvet voice, this time tinged with such tenderness, made her want things he wouldn't give her.

She wanted to turn and see those broad shoulders and strong arms above the rim, his knees raised above the water. But what she desperately craved and what he'd solemnly vowed were two very different things.

He did not love her. He wouldn't allow himself to.

"Stay with me," he whispered.

Chapter Eleven

JOHN THOUGHT SHE MIGHT excuse herself, as she waited an awful long time to accept his invitation. He realized he was a mite selfish to ask her to stay. She was probably exhausted. But he'd been so filled with hope when she'd still been awake upon his return.

He needed to talk to her.

He needed her companionship.

He needed Millie. Not a comfortable thought, but it was the truth.

I love this woman, my wife.

After a long moment she finally turned, her features bronzed in firelight. "Of course." She seemed unsure of this new intimacy. Unsure where to let her eyes rest, unsure where to stand or sit.

He wanted to make this easy for her. "Come back to the rocker. Finish drying your hair." He soaped his upper body, washed his neck and face. Cupped water to pour over his head.

She might be trying to keep her gaze from him, but wasn't doing the best job of it.

He found her modesty endearing.

He knew for a fact she'd seen a man before. Oliver was proof of that.

But she hadn't seen him.

She looked at him then with appreciation and fascination she couldn't hide—good. Her interest felt good.

He wanted her hands on him, craved her touch with a hunger he didn't want to deny. "Wash my hair?"

That slight smile again, so beautiful it made his heart roll over in his chest. In the firelight, in that moment, she'd never been so lovely.

She pushed up the sleeves of her nightgown, knelt behind the tub, and dipped into the pot of soft soap.

The sensation of her fingers working the lather through his hair, massaging his scalp, was at once both splendid and tortuous. He clenched his jaw to hold back a moan of pleasure. She pulled the suds through the length of his hair.

He'd thought she might speak, if only to diminish the potency of this intimacy—but she remained silent. He wished he could see her features, read her, see what this meant to her.

The gentle drag of fingertips over his scalp, from brow and temple to crown and nape raised gooseflesh on his arms. He closed his eyes to savor the pleasurable sensations of her touch.

As the simple task of washing his hair stretched to twice the time he normally spent, and held his tongue—no way would he interrupt her. Too soon she dipped a tin cup into the tub and poured water over his head to rinse the lather away. Still, she worked her fingers through his hair as she poured yet another cup of water, ensuring no trace of soap remained.

With both hands, she wrung the excessive water from his hair, twisting it into a single rope. He didn't want her to leave him and was just about to say so when she took the wet cloth she'd draped over the edge of the tub from her own bath, soaped it, and gently nudged his shoulder. "Lean forward."

She washed his back, the strokes sure and efficient, but at the same time glorious. Her touch had awakened in him longings he'd believed lost with Abigail. How had he ever thought he'd never desire another? He'd foolishly believed his heart so full with love for Abby, that there wouldn't be room for anyone else.

Obviously, he'd been wrong.

At least he could honestly admit his love for Abigail hadn't been lost—she'd been his first love, the wife of his youth, the mother of his children, and he loved her still. But Millie had enlarged his broken heart, making ample room for herself there, too. It seemed good, right, that he loved Millie, too. How could he not?

Millie wrung out the cloth, draped it back over the edge of the tub, and stood. Already, he missed her touch.

She resumed combing her hair at the heat of the fire.

Reluctantly, he broke the companionable, intimate silence. "I finished the job outside." She would know he referred to the burial. He soaped up his lower body, scrubbed off the sweat and grime. "I'll show you where, should you like to know for young Oliver's sake."

"Thank you." She turned her gaze back to the fire in the hearth. "I can't imagine wanting to sit at his graveside."

Her eyes met his readily enough. He didn't glimpse pain in those clear eyes, nor guilt.

Something else simmered there. Hope? Interest...in him?

That moment seemed to slow to an unnatural crawl. He held Millie's gaze and ached to blurt his newfound feelings. Surely she witnessed that truth. He was helpless to contain it, to hide it from her. He closed his eyes.

She must've glimpsed the truth, because she touched his forearm where it rested on the tub's edge. He opened his eyes to find her kneeling there, her long hair casting shadows from firelight across her features. He glimpsed concern and love in her eyes.

Before he thought it through, he'd covered her hand on his arm. *Don't go.*

Would it be so bad to welcome all the risks inherent in loving this wife? To grab whatever little time he had with her, be it a few days, a dozen years, or the rest of his miserable life?

She knelt so close he could feel the gentle caress of her breath fan his cheek.

No, it wouldn't be so bad.

He wanted to love her, wanted to take the leap.

He leaned near, watching her closely for any sign she

wasn't ready or didn't feel the way he did. Her eyes widened just a little as his intentions registered.

To his delight, she met him halfway.

Her lips touched his so tentatively, so softly, he instantly craved more. He wanted to cup her head and hold her fast so he could kiss her properly. Instead, he reveled in the gentleness of this first kiss. Patience was rewarded when she increased the pressure all on her own.

Too soon she broke that kiss. She pulled back and searched his expression.

He imagined she could see the longing and love and surrender that fairly overwhelmed him. He wanted more. He wanted the freedom to kiss his wife, to hold her near. He wanted everything—her affection, her love, her heart.

He wanted forever.

She didn't need to say the words. He could read her emotion so clearly on her beautiful face. How had he ever thought her plain?

Confident she'd come to love him, too, John spoke the words he hoped would change everything between them for the better. "It seems my heart's bigger than I thought, Millie, with plenty of room there for *you*. I love you."

Her smile came so quick, so naturally. A man couldn't ask for a better reaction.

He rushed forward, eager to say all that was in his heart. "I'm sorry I vowed *not* to."

It seemed she was unwilling to keep her distance. With that, she drew near and rested her cheek against his. Satin against damp rough-hewn wood. He knew his beard stubble must chafe her skin. Mindful, he held still, holding her little hand.

He waited, wanting to hear her say she loved him, but the words didn't come.

He wouldn't press it. She hadn't been able to hide the feelings...he'd seen them where they mattered most, so truthful in her eyes. Maybe, in time, she would speak the words.

He could exercise patience.

"I love you," he repeated, softly, so near her ear. "Will you truly be my wife? In name only isn't enough. Not anymore. I want you to be mine."

TEARS SLIPPED DOWN MILLIE'S CHEEKS. Oh, how John's words touched her soul. She doubted she could get a word past the emotion constricting her throat.

So she nodded, the bristles on his cheek abrading her own. His touch felt wonderful. So right, so welcome.

They'd already said their vows, they were man and wife—John had accepted her as such even before Oliver's demise. And now he confessed loving her. Why, in the face of her unworthiness, she'd never understand, yet believed he told the truth.

John's lips nuzzled her cheek, her ear.

She fairly melted against him. How desperate, this need for his affection, his love, his touch.

She hadn't known how badly she needed it until he'd offered.

"Stay with me tonight." He whispered the request, but she felt it echoing in her soul as if he'd shouted.

There could be no misunderstanding him. And how she desperately wanted to be his wife, in every way.

And she was ready—almost. Before she went to his bed, she simply had to tell him of her suspicion that she was with child.

He deserves to know.

It would be so easy to let her love for her husband carry her to his bed, to his arms, and keep this secret. After all, she might *not* be with child. It wasn't exactly lying to withhold the suspicion. Then, if she did conceive, the babe would be John's.

His soft ministrations of his lips upon her cheek gradually moved to her jaw. Two kisses became three.

With her pulse pounding in her ears, she felt so tempted to grab this moment, to wait another week, maybe two, for the difficult conversation. If she put it off, they'd have time to become closer, to solidify their marriage, so that when he did learn, he might not care as much that she carried Oliver's seed.

The mere thought of Oliver made her shiver. Had that man *ever* kissed her with such gentle ministrations? Even in those few short days before the war? Ever *once* during their courtship?

It wasn't right to compare the two men. John was a prince to Oliver's miscreant.

Oh, how she wanted to hold her tongue and accept everything John offered.

But it was he who kindled the desire to be better, infinitely better, than she'd been before him. A desperation to prove her worthiness to her husband wouldn't allow her to wait.

She had to tell him.

Now.

John remained silent, allowing kisses to do the persuading. Millie fairly melted against him. He longed to stand and pull her flush against him.

But this was enough—for the moment.

He'd felt her sigh against him. Thinking this through, no doubt. He knew she'd reached some sort of a decision when she stilled and squeezed the hand she held.

Slowly, she eased back, just enough to look him in the eye. A shy smile lifted her mouth, softened her expression. His heart nearly exploded with the tender love he glimpsed there.

Oh, yeah. His wife loved him.

And it felt darn good.

Still tears trailed down her cheeks. He'd felt the hot moisture against his skin minutes ago, but these sure looked like tears of happiness. He released her hand to move a thumb to her cheek, drying the track. She turned to his palm, pressed a light kiss there.

"Yes," she murmured.

"Yes?" He palmed the edge of the tub, pulled his feet beneath him to push out of the water, grab the towel and—

She stopped him with two hands, held out in a simple gesture.

Sadness marred her features, chasing away the bliss he'd so cherished.

"First," she said so softly he barely heard, "before…"

Several heartbeats passed. He searched his bride's face, trying to figure out what the problem was. She seemed agonized. If she didn't want to come to his bed, he wouldn't force her. She knew that, didn't she?

"I suspect..." She cleared her throat. "It's probable, but I'm not sure, of course."

His brows drew together as he tried to grasp the meaning behind her vague confession. "What?"

"I don't know for certain—but I think I'm—" she drew a shaky breath, "I'm with child."

Three simple words slammed into him as if he'd been thrown from a horse. Fear knocked the breath clean out of him. *Pregnant?*

He closed his eyes against the rising tide of memories. Images of Abigail, wasting away, her belly huge with that fourth pregnancy, her cheeks sunken and her will to live all but washed away.

The birthing had been...difficult.

Abigail, screaming, so weakly, in the pains of labor. Her pale blond hair matted to her head with sweat. Abigail, her face turned away from their newborn daughter. Rejecting that precious baby girl as her life barely began.

Alone, he'd named the babe Sarah Abigail. He'd taken the squalling baby into the settlement to find a wet nurse when it became evident Abigail wouldn't. *Couldn't.*

He had sapped her will to live, to defy the cancer. Four births in less than three years.

And now Millie.

Though rationally, he knew he must separate the two—Millie potentially carried Oliver's child, not his. Abigail had contracted cancer—a piece of rotten luck outside his control—and Millie seemed healthy. He felt helpless, realizing he didn't know how whether her first delivery had been easy or difficult.

What if he lost her?

She still spoke, haltingly, and he realized he'd missed much of what she'd said. "...at least I think so. You deserve to know."

What was he doing?

How could he so easily have forgotten all the reasons why this marriage had to *stay* in name only?

He couldn't breathe under the unbearable weight of guilt.

He could not stay here, beneath Millie's watchful gaze.

She wanted a response, and he couldn't give her one. What was he supposed to say? That he wouldn't take her to his bed? If he did, his love for her would deepen, solidify, redouble...and when he lost her—whether in childbirth or an uncontrollable fate—he doubted he'd survive it.

Losing Abby had devastated him; he sensed losing Millie would utterly destroy him.

Without a thought for her sensibilities, he surged to his feet, splashing bath water over the rim. He grabbed for the towel and wrapped it about his hips. Water streamed down his body as he stepped out of the tub and bent to grab the clothing she'd laid out for him.

Without looking back, he slammed the door behind himself, barely in time to mask the sob that escaped his throat.

Chapter Twelve

THREE LONG DAYS PASSED in John's silence.

Millie kept her chin up, went through the motions of keeping house, tending to the needs of the children, cooking, putting up the last of the garden's vegetables and turning its soil in preparation for winter.

In her sleeplessness, she completed two new shirts for John.

And forbade tears.

She refused to allow his silence to break her. But it was so incredibly difficult to know what might have been between them—a real marriage.

He spent all day in the fields, returning long after she and the children had gone to bed. The only way she knew he'd returned after that first long day was his dinner plate scraped clean and evidence he'd eaten breakfast and refilled his lunch pail.

John's avoidance and rejection brought back all the old feelings of unworthiness he'd helped put to rest, mere days ago. John had helped her see the truth of that matter—those failings belonged to Oliver. Still, John's rejection hurt far more than anything Oliver had ever done, for one singularly powerful reason; she loved John as she'd *never* loved Oliver.

She couldn't fully understand why he didn't want her.

She'd thought over the abrupt and disastrous conclusion to that night's conversation, the result of her confession that sent him running from the house and her presence.

He didn't want her. Because he didn't want Oliver's child growing within her? No other assumption made any sense.

Worthless. Useless. Oliver's taunts echoed in her mind. After all, she couldn't bear John a child until she'd delivered Oliver's. *Good-for-nothing.*

She hated the way Oliver's degradation made her view herself. How long had she carried that shame in her heart, burned into her soul like a brand?

Too long, but no more.

Never again. She would not revert to the old patterns. She loved John Gideon, and he loved her. She'd earned his love, deserved it. He'd helped her embrace that truth. He wouldn't be rid of her so easily.

On the morning of the fourth day, Millie rose with new resolve.

She would put an end to John's silence, and she would do it now.

He'd tried to move about in the main room quietly, but she'd heard the whisper of his footfalls, the soft sounds of him rolling up his pallet, the muted scrape of knife slicing bread.

She stepped out of the bedroom to find he'd quit the house.

Frustration welled within her.

That man had claimed to love her. Love did not present itself as a silent, cold shoulder. Love did not ignore, reject, judge, nor neglect.

Love did not wound—not like this. If her first marriage had taught her anything, it taught her the stark difference between what love was and was not.

She'd learned far more from her second marriage, from the time spent in Kansas, with John. Far from the same woman who arrived, bruised and starving, she'd learned to handle a rifle with confidence. Realized hard work should be appreciated and admired between a husband and wife, and what it truly meant to be in a marriage partnership.

Heavens, she'd stood up to a threat, even killed in

defense of her own life and the lives of her children. She'd grown, changed, cast off the shackles of her life with Oliver. Blast John's pride or fear or whatever it was that made him think she was too weak to face the problem—he couldn't keep this to himself a moment longer.

She would not allow it.

In the past, she had not deserved Oliver's beatings, and now, she did not deserve John's indifference and silence.

She sighed in frustration as she returned to her room where she rolled on stockings and buttoned on shoes. Wrapped Abigail's hand-me-down shawl about her shoulders. These lost minutes gave John ample time to get too far away from the house.

He'd hung the triangle, though it served little to no purpose now. She thought about ringing it with a vengeance to bring him running.

If he came at all.

On the porch, she picked up the beater, considering whether this was how she wanted to wage this particular scrimmage.

In the light of the setting moon, she found John standing in the family cemetery at Abigail's grave, shoulders slumped and hat in his hands.

Her anger evaporated.

He dropped to his knees where he'd buried Abigail and his pain mingled with her own, intensifying.

There was more to this than the simple news she was with child, honestly, by her first husband.

Did he grapple with guilt over a growing love for her, Millie, while he still loved Abigail? Did he believe more time should have passed since Abigail's death?

Slowly, frustration ebbed, leaving determination in its wake. Her marriage to John Gideon was worth saving.

A scant minute later, she stood at his shoulder. He hadn't moved from where he knelt. He must have seen and heard her approaching. The early morning was hush and still.

She waited a long moment, allowing him time to compose himself. Seeing him like this dissolved any remaining antagonism right along with the anger.

But they were still going to talk. She needed to

understand him, if they'd have any chance of living together peaceably.

She knelt at his side. Not quite touching him, but close enough to feel the heat of his body. She heard his breath, so uneven and ragged.

A chill wind whipped past, cutting easily through her clothing, eliciting a shiver.

When long moments passed and he hadn't spoken, Millie did. "John. Talk to me."

He sighed. "Abigail died soon after giving birth to Sarah."

He'd written as much in his letter. He'd told her so, that first morning after they wed. And recently, he'd told her of the cancer. "Yes."

He sat, propping his arms over his raised knees and fisted both hands into his hair. "I killed her, Mil."

His agony sliced through her as if it were her own. "You said she died from cancer."

"Oh, I may not have put my hands about her throat, but bringing her here, getting four children on her in less than three years, crushed the life out of her just the same. She didn't have the strength to fight the growing tumor."

His guilt was a palpable thing. She couldn't bear to hear him suffer like this.

"The doctor said the cancer's growth was accelerated by her pregnancies. If she hadn't been with child—"

Settling herself beside him, Millie dared to rest her head on his shoulder, put a gentle hand on his arm. "I'm so sorry you lost her. I see how dearly you love her." It broke her heart, knowing this man she loved so completely grieved a dead woman, loved the one he'd lost more than he could ever love her.

Oh, he might have wanted her, but he didn't love her the way he loved Abigail. Slowly, she sat upright, her hand lingering on his arm.

"She was never the same after our silent son." He gestured with a shoulder to a little grassy mound beside Abigail's. "The other children came along, too soon, too many of them, and she just gave up. I tried to help her, tried to give her strength, but she wasted away. I'm surprised she lived long enough to see Sarah into the world."

The forlorn emptiness within John broke Millie's heart. She wondered how long the cancer had been present in Abigail's body, if the illness had eroded her health from the beginning, as early as that first pregnancy. It made more sense than not.

No matter what the doctor said, Millie found no fault in John, but it seemed the wrong time to voice her certainty.

He pushed to his feet and offered her a hand up.

He held her hand, threading their fingers together as he led the way back toward the house. He seemed unwilling to look at her as he said, "I'm scared. You're at risk." He swallowed hard. "You could die."

Her footsteps stalled. He worried about *her*?

As he squeezed her hand, and at last met her gaze, the overwhelming guilt she glimpsed there caught her unprepared. She hadn't realized it devoured him.

She stepped into his embrace and pulled him close. He came easily, locking his arms about her with a kind of desperation.

"I can't lose you," he whispered.

"I'm here."

"But for how long? I couldn't bear it if you're only mine for a little while and then gone."

So that's why he'd pulled away, remained stoically silent for three long, miserable days. Out of fear that *when* he lost her—*not if*—he'd suffer that much more. *If* he allowed himself to love her.

Understanding him, irrational fears and all, made her love him all the more. "Let's not borrow trouble."

He shrugged, as if he couldn't dismiss his concerns so easily.

"I'm healthy as a horse. I'll likely outlive you."

That brought out a wry smile. "I'd almost prefer it that way."

The bleakness in his brown eyes sobered her. She glimpsed his pain over losing family members to death—she couldn't blame him, not really, for praying he'd not have to experience the like again. "I'm glad you don't want to lose me."

"It's true."

"My pregnancy with young Oliver was easy. The midwife said my labor was shorter and easier than most first-time mothers'. She said I'm built to have babies."

"You're so small." He took her hips in his hands, as if measuring the width and proving his point.

"Didn't matter. Childbirth was easy, and it *will* be easy, again."

That promise seemed to calm John a little more, but she didn't like the tension showing about his eyes and in the clenching of his jaw. Lamplight spilled through the window, casting enough illumination over his handsome face that she couldn't miss the doubt carved on those dear features.

"Try not to worry." She pushed up on her toes to kiss his lips.

He tightened his hold on her, returning her kiss with fervor.

When he at last broke their kiss, she said, "You're done ghosting in and out of the house in the middle of the night. You hear me? You are done avoiding me, John. That hurt, because I love you."

His expression turned contrite. He cupped the back of her neck in his hand and kissed her cheek. "I'm sorry, Mil. Forgive me?"

"Yes." She paused, still needing to know, desperately, how he felt about the probability that she'd bring another of Oliver's children into the world. "Do you forgive me?"

"Hmm?" He pressed a kiss to her jaw.

"If I'm carrying Oliver's child."

"There's nothing to forgive. I'm just scared. That's all. Terrified of losing you when I've just found you."

Millie pulled away, took her husband's dear face in her hands, and forced him to meet her gaze. The eastern sky was lighter now, showing the faint strains of pink and lavender that heralded a new day. A fresh start.

"Life is precious," she told him, "We might have thirty years, three weeks or a mere three days. With or without more babies."

He nodded, as if at least intellectually, he understood that to be true.

"It's true—I had a healthy confinement, an easy delivery

bringing young Oliver into the world. I want us to have children together. I want to give you that—more sons to carry your name and help you work this land, daughters with your brown eyes and quick smile. Even more, I want to show you that together, we're strong enough to bring children into our home and love them and welcome them with rejoicing."

John pulled her with him to the front porch where he sat in the lone chair and settled her onto his lap, draping her legs over his thighs. He encircled her waist and snuggled her close.

"Sounds like you want to amend our agreement," he kissed her brow, "Mrs. Gideon."

She nodded, relishing his gentle ministrations. His touch warmed her clear through. She looped her arms about his neck, savoring their newfound closeness.

He kissed one eyelid, then the other. "You want to be my wife, not just my bride."

"Yes." She sought his mouth, kissed him thoroughly.

He pulled away too soon. "Anything else you want to tell me?"

She opened her eyes, searched his face, not quite comprehending.

"You've knocked me out of the saddle, twice. First, with news your not-yet-deceased husband knew where you'd gone and my family was in danger—and you were in danger too, by the way—and second, that you're breeding."

"*Might* be." She chuckled. His tone held no criticism, not one bit of angst. She loved this about him. "You know all my secrets."

He raised a brow. "I do?"

"Every last one. Including the fact I've fallen in love with you."

His grin came quick and easy, tugging on her healing heart.

"Anything else *you* want to tell *me*, Mr. Gideon?"

"Yes, ma'am."

Her heart thudded. She couldn't read his expression. Was he playing or serious?

"I," he kissed her lips, "love," another peck, "you."

She signed with happiness. "I already knew that."

Releasing his hold about her middle, he settled a big palm over her belly. "And for the record, any children born within the bonds of our marriage are *mine*."

Chapter Thirteen

Epilogue

December, 1871

AS IT TURNED OUT, A BABY *WAS* BORN to them. A full thirteen months after Oliver's death.

Thirteen sweet months during which the children grew and seemed to have forgotten any inkling of that awful day.

Millie had seen the best of John during their year of marriage. All the children—including young Oliver—had a loving, protective father who bounced them on his knee, carried them on broad shoulders, and told bedtime stories. It warmed Millie's heart to hear Oliver call John papa.

She thought she couldn't be more in love with him, but the moment she handed the sweet bundle of newborn baby boy into her husband's waiting hands, she realized the possibility.

John Gideon deserved all the love she could lavish on him.

And he'd brought out the best in her. She'd felt more honored, cherished, and valued than ever before. John had given that gift of confidence.

Sitting on a chair at Millie's bedside, his big hands cradling their tightly swaddled infant, John's expression softened with love and a great deal of relief.

The midwife slipped out of the new bedroom John had built, closing the door behind her. In the main room, the children giggled and little voices demanded to see the new baby. Snug log walls kept the winter wind at bay. A cheery fire burned in the bedroom hearth.

Millie touched John's dear face, his hair as soft as flour. "What will you call him?"

Her hand moved to his shoulder. She felt the tightness he still carried in his muscles from the terror he'd experienced during the labor. Even though that labor had been less than two hours in duration. He'd barely had time to ride for the midwife and return with her before the baby was born.

"Other than *mine?*"

She laughed. It seemed happiness was a given these days. "Yes. But he needs a name."

"I thought he'd be a girl. I haven't even considered boys' names. What do you want to call him?"

"I want him to have your name. Let's call him John."

"Oh, no. Too confusing." The baby fussed in his arms, and he snuggled the little bundle against his chest, soothing like the experienced father he was. "I like to hear my name on your lips too much to wonder if you're speaking to me or this young'un."

With the muted giggles of their little ones playing together in the next room, and the babe's safe delivery behind them, Millie didn't know if she could hold much more happiness.

"Jack, then? After you?" She watched him closely for signs of whether he liked the idea or not.

"My father's name was Jonathan."

She smiled. "Jonathan it is."

He lay their baby in her arms. "Rest now. I need to see you regain your health. Quickly."

She'd seen the flicker of fear in his eyes when he'd entered the bedroom to squalls of his newborn son, how his eyes had searched her, measuring her strength, her will. "Yes, dear."

He kissed her brow. "I love you, Permilia Gideon."

She snuggled their son close, looked up at her husband and saw unmistakable love shining strong and precious in his eyes.

How very blessed, to have found this good man, to be surrounded by his goodness and love and light. Her heart was so very full.

"And I love you, John Gideon."

~ THE END ~

Please *share* this book with a friend.
Paperback books are easy to loan.

Please *recommend* this book.
*Please share your thoughts on this book
with friends.*

Please post a *review*.
*Reviews from readers make all the difference to those
browsing and buying, as well as to writers. Please take a
moment and leave an honest review—
as few as 20 words will do.*

on Amazon.com

http://amzn.to/1nxpRe4
(case sensitive)

*and
on Goodreads.com*

http://bit.ly/1jytLP3
(case sensitive)

Home for Christmas

A Sweet Historical Romance Novella
(Rated G)

by Kristin Holt

Miranda sneaks home after a long absence, determined to avoid her former fiance. But Hunter wants far more than his old role as brother-in-law-to-be. Abundant Christmas spirit, matchmaking mothers, and hometown holiday celebrations conspire against Miranda's plans for a quiet, at-home Christmas.

Her heart doesn't stand a chance.

Home for Christmas

is available as an eBook at various online retailers—

At Amazon.com
http://amzn.to/1fcxAOj
(case sensitive)

And BN.com
http://bit.ly/1jfsLDP
(case sensitive)

~and~
also in paperback,

At Amazon.com
http://amzn.to/1iitikl
(case sensitive)

At BN.com
http://bit.ly/1jfsLDP
(case sensitive)

The Bride Lottery

A Sweet Historical Mail Order Bride Romance (Rated PG)

**Forty Bachelors.
Fifteen Brides.
What could go wrong?**

Evelyn is in a pickle.

In less than five months, Evelyn Brandt will be an unwed mother. Her parents discover her secret and send her away on the next west-bound train. They insist she deliver the child on the other side of the continent where the disgrace won't harm her father's business empire and the family's social standing. She'll be allowed to return home after the child is adopted by decent people *and* her corset fits properly once more.

Sam's in charge of the Bride Lottery, and the competition's fierce.

It's too bad the mail order bride agency failed to round up even half their order, 'cause every man on the mountain wants a bride—except Sam Kochler—so he's saddled with enforcing the rules. He received bios of each lady the agency sent, so when Evelyn steps off the train, he's a tad curious and a mite too interested.

The tougher the competition becomes, the worse some fellas behave, and it's not long before Sam finds himself courting Evelyn—only to protect her while she makes up her mind. He won't allow himself to fall in love and still doesn't want a wife...or so he keeps telling himself.

The Bride Lottery

Is available as an ebook at Amazon.com

http://amzn.com/B00MACH28Y

Paperback edition coming soon!

Books by Kristin Holt
please see

www.KristinHolt.com

And while you're there, please sign up for a newsletter, to *be the first to hear about new releases.*

About the Author

Kristin's love of books and reading began as a preschooler. She arrived home after her first day of Kindergarten frustrated to tears that they hadn't taught her to read (though her parents already had). Today, she devours several books a week, always searching for more authors to add to her keeper shelf. The advent of eBooks made that keeper shelf take up significantly less room, thus ensuring her husband is less aware of the book addiction.

Kristin has worked as a Registered Nurse (Labor and Delivery, Maternal-Child), Childbirth Educator, magazine article writer, Weight Watchers Territory Manager and Leader. Through it all, writing remained her first love. She lives north of Salt Lake City with her husband of twenty-five years, three college-age kids who haven't completely moved out, a daughter dancing her way through high school, and a Vizsla named Snickerdoodle.

Find her at www.KristinHolt.com.

Printed in Great Britain
by Amazon